# the darkest SUNRISE

The Darkest Sunrise Duet 1

ALY MARTINEZ

Sticks and stones will break my bones, but *words* will never harm me.

Whoever coined that phrase is a bald-faced liar. *Words* are often the sharpest weapon of all, triggering some of the most powerful emotions a human can experience.

"You're pregnant."

"It's a boy."

"Your son needs a heart transplant."

Sticks and stones will break my bones, but words will never harm me.

*Lies.*

Syllables and letters may not be tangible, but they can still destroy your entire life faster than a bullet from a gun.

Two words—that was all it took to extinguish the sun from my sky.

"He's gone."

For ten years, the darkness consumed me.

In the end, it was four deep, gravelly *words* that gave me hope of another sunrise.

"Hi. I'm Porter Reese."

*The Darkest Sunrise*


Cover Designer: Jay Aheer
Photography: Wander Aguiar
Editing: Mickey Reed
Formatting: Stacey Blake

# the darkest SUNRISE

The Darkest Sunrise Duet 1

# PROLOGUE

## Charlotte

STICKS AND STONES WILL BREAK MY BONES, BUT WORDS will never harm me.

Whoever coined that phrase is a bald-faced liar. Words are often the sharpest weapons of all, triggering some of the most powerful emotions a human can experience.

"You're pregnant," were not the *words* I wanted to hear when I was starting my first year of medical school.

Yes, I was well acquainted with how the whole reproductive system worked, but a drunken one-night stand with a man I'd met exactly one hour earlier wasn't supposed to end with a broken condom and me carrying his baby.

"It's a boy," the doctor said as she placed that bloody, beautiful mess on my chest nine months later.

I wasn't positive his gargled wail could be considered a *word* at all, but that sound changed my entire life. One glance in those gray, unfocused eyes and I wasn't just a reluctant woman who'd had a baby. I was a *mother* on a primal level.

Heart. Soul. Eternally.

"Lucas," I whispered as I held all seven pounds and two ounces of the little boy who was forever mine to protect. I knew down to the marrow of my bones that there was nothing I wouldn't do for him. But, as I would learn so many times over the years that followed, not everything was in my control.

"Your son will eventually need a heart transplant," the doctor said as we anxiously sat in a cardiologist's office after a long night in the emergency room. In that moment, I could have given Lucas mine, because with those *words*, it felt as though my heart had been ripped straight from my chest. I was well aware that not every child was the picture of perfect health. But he was *mine*. I'd grown him inside my body from nothing more than a cluster of dividing cells and into an incredible, tiny human who would one day blaze his own path through this crazy world.

Ten fingers. Ten toes. My raven hair. His father's dimpled chin. That baby had gone from something I never wanted to the only thing I needed. I refused to accept that he could be sick.

After the doctor walked away, Brady stared at me from across the room, our son tucked against his chest, and assaulted me with more *words*.

"They can fix him, right?"

But it was my reply that cut the deepest.

"No."

I knew too much about Lucas's diagnosis to believe that anyone could *fix* him. One day, likely before his eighteenth birthday, his frail heart would give out and I'd be forced to helplessly watch the sole reason for my existence struggle to survive. He'd be added to a mile-long donor registry and we'd start the agonizing—and morally exhausting—task of waiting for someone to die so our child could live.

Knowledge was not power in that situation. I'd have given anything to be ignorant to what the doctor's *words* meant for us.

Hundreds of people on that donor registry would die before they were ever matched. And that's not to mention the ones who'd die on the table or those who'd reject the organ and pass away within hours of receiving it. In medical school, we prided ourselves in the statistics of people we saved. But this was *my* son. He had only one life. I couldn't risk that he'd lose it.

That *I'd* lose *him*.

Through my devastation, I attempted to remain positive. I faked smiles, pretending to accept *words* of encouragement from our friends and family, and I even managed to offer Brady a few inspirational *words* of my own. He didn't bother offering any in return. We didn't have that kind of relationship. Turned out, fully clothed, we had little in common. However, after Lucas was born, we'd become something that resembled friends. And, with the prospect of a future spent in and out of hospitals on our hands, that bond strengthened.

That is, until six months later, when one innocent *word* ruined us all.

Sticks and stones will break my bones, but words will never harm me.

Lies.

Syllables and letters may not be tangible, but they can still destroy your entire life faster than a bullet from a gun.

One word.

That was all it took to extinguish the sun from my sky.

"Shhh," I cooed, reaching over the stroller handle to push the pacifier hanging from a blue-and-white-polka-dot ribbon, monogrammed with his name, back into his mouth.

He'd been in a mood all night. It seemed being six months old was an impossible job. I couldn't imagine the pure torture of an all-you-can-eat milk buffet and a team of people responding to your every whim—including when said whims were nothing more than to puke or pee on aforementioned people.

It was the first morning of fall, but the sweltering Atlanta summer still lingered in the air. Between clinicals and Lucas's nonexistent sleep schedule, I was barely clinging to consciousness.

My boy loved being outside, and I loved the way it made him drowsy regardless of how hard he fought. So, with hopes that we'd both be able to sneak in a morning nap, I'd strapped him into the obnoxiously expensive stroller Brady's mother had bought me for my baby shower and taken him for a walk through the local park.

That quaint playground less than half a mile from our house was one of my favorite places in the world and exactly why I commuted the extra fifteen minutes to school every day. I enjoyed watching the children play while imagining what it would be like when Lucas was that age. Images of him racing across the monkey bars to escape a horde of giggling little girls paraded through my mind, making me smile. Would he be social like me? Quiet and reserved like Brady? Or sick, stuck in a hospital, waiting on a heart that might never come? I pushed those thoughts out of my head when a desperate shriek from a woman stopped me in my tracks.

"Help!"

One *word.*

I stepped on the brake of the stroller and whirled to face her, my throat constricting as she lifted a limp toddler off the ground.

A blast of adrenaline shot through my system, and on instinct, I sprinted the few yards over to her.

"He's not breathing!" she cried, frantically transferring her lifeless child into my open arms.

"Call nine-one-one," I ordered. My pulse quickened as I laid his small body on the top of a picnic table, years of training flooding my mind in a jumbled mess. "What happened?" I asked, tipping his head back to check his airway and finding it open, but no breath was flowing through it.

"I…I don't know," she stammered. "He just fell… Oh God! He's not breathing!"

"Calm down," I barked. Though I wasn't completely sure which one of us I was talking to. It was my first emergency situation, and while I was a hell of a lot better than anyone else in that park, if I'd been in her situation, I would have wanted someone more qualified to be standing over Lucas.

But, as a group of moms congregated around us, not a single one stepping forward to offer help, I was all she had. So, with my heart in my throat, I went to work, praying that I was enough.

Within a matter of minutes, a weak cry streamed from the boy's blue lips.

His mother's sob of relief was a sound I would never forget. Deep, as though it had originated in her soul and merely exited through her mouth.

"Oh God!" she screamed, her hands shaking as she bent over his stirring body to tuck his face against her neck.

As his cries grew louder, I inched away to give him some space. I couldn't tear my gaze away from the miracle of this child who had, minutes earlier, been nothing more than a vacant body. Now, he was clinging to the neck of his mother.

With a quivering chin and tears pricking the backs of my eyes, I smiled to myself. I'd been struggling. Balancing the rigors of med school and the self-doubt of being a single mother was hard enough, but combined with twelve-hour days only to come home and study for six more, I was fading fast. I'd gone so far as to contemplate taking a few years off until Lucas got a little older.

As the paramedics arrived, I basked in the knowledge that all of my hard work and sacrifice had bought a little boy a second chance at life. In that moment, all the reasons why I'd wanted to become a doctor in the first place came flooding back.

Pablo Picasso once said, "The meaning of life is to find your gift. The purpose of life is to give it away."

I'd known from the tender age of seven when my next-door neighbor had skinned her knee and I'd splinted her leg before going to get her mom that medicine was my gift.

It was time for me to give that gift away to others who needed it.

"Thank you," the frazzled mother called out to me as I backed away, a newfound resolve invigorating me.

I simply nodded and placed my hand over my racing heart, feeling as though I should be the one thanking her.

When I lost sight of her behind the wall of first responders and Nosy-Nellies, I turned on a toe and headed back to Lucas's stroller.

Only to come to a screeching halt less than a second later.

He wasn't there.

I scanned the area, assuming I'd gotten turned around during the chaos. But, after a few seconds, it hit me. Something was wrong.

Terribly, earth-shatteringly wrong.

"Lucas," I called as if my six-month-old were going to answer me.

He didn't.

In fact, no one did.

The hairs on the back of my neck stood on end, and my pulse skyrocketed. The world moved in slow motion around me as I spun in a circle. My mind reeled with possibilities of where he could be. But, even in that moment of terror, I knew with an absolute certainty that I'd left him right there, buckled safely into his stroller, only a few yards away.

"Lucas!" I yelled, my anxiety soaring to immeasurable heights.

With frantic movements, I jogged over to the slowly dispersing crowd.

I caught a woman's arm before she could pass me. "Have you seen my son?"

Her eyes startled, but she shook her head.

I scrambled to the next woman. "Have you seen my son?"

She too shook her head, so I kept going, grabbing people and begging they would finally nod.

"Green stroller. Navy Trim?"

Another headshake.

My vision tunneled and my throat burned, but I never stopped moving.

He was there. Somewhere. He had to be.

My heart slammed into my ribs as yet another rush of adrenaline—and what I feared was reality—ravaged my body.

"Lucas!" I screamed.

My thoughts became jumbled, and I lost all sense of rationality. I raced to the first stroller I saw. It was pink with white polka dots, but he could have been inside.

"Hey!" a woman yelled as I snatched the blanket off her baby.

*Her baby.* Not mine.

"Lucas!"

Bile burned a trail of fire up my throat. With every passing second, my terror amplified. I raked a hand into my hair as the paralyzing helplessness dug its claws into me and threatened to drag me down to my knees. I forced myself to stay on my feet.

For him, I'd do anything.

"Lucas!" I choked one last time, a wave of trembles rolling through me.

*One word.*

It had worked for her. That other woman. When she had been desperate and at risk of losing her son, I'd given him back to her.

Someone would do that for me.

They had to.

"Help!" I screamed at the top of my lungs.

*One word.*

And then my entire world went dark.

# ONE

## Porter

"DADDY?"

*Yeah,* I thought, but I was too deep in sleep to force the words out. It had been weeks since I'd gotten any real rest. Between work and the kids, I was beyond exhausted.

"Daddy?"

*Right here, baby.*

"Daddy!" she yelled.

I bolted upright in bed, groggily searching the room.

She stood in the doorway, her long, chestnut hair in tangles, and the silly Hello Kitty nightgown she'd insisted on sleeping in every day for the last week brushed the hardwood floor.

"What's wrong, Hannah?" I asked, using the heels of my palms to scrub the sleep from my eyes.

"Travis can't breathe."

Three words that birthed my nightmares, haunted my

dreams, and lived in my reality.

Slinging the covers back, I flew from the bed. My bare feet pounded against the floor as I rushed down the hall to his bedroom.

Hannah had started sleeping with him weeks earlier. Her big brother acted like it was a cruel and unusual form of torture, but secretly, I thought he liked having the company.

And, while she was three and a half, it still made me feel worlds better that someone was with him on nights like this.

Pushing his door wide, careful not to rip the Minecraft poster we'd hung up earlier in the day, I hurried to his bed only to find it empty.

"Trav?" I called.

It was Hannah who answered. "He's in the bathroom."

I kicked a box of Legos out of my way and opened the bottom drawer on his nightstand to retrieve his nebulizer. Suddenly, an avalanche of empty Gatorade bottles tumbled down from the top bunk.

As I rushed from the room, a bolt of pride struck me. That was my boy. Sick as hell, stuck in bed for the last week, and he'd somehow managed to find the energy to booby-trap his room.

"Hey," I whispered as I turned the corner into the hall bathroom.

My stomach knotted at the sight. His thin body was perched on the edge of the tub, his shoulders hunched over and his elbows resting on his thighs. He was drenched in sweat, and his color was off. Deep, labored breaths not making it to his lungs rounded his back with every inhale.

"Please…no," he heaved.

I knew what he was asking, but I was in no position to promise him anything.

"Shhh, I got ya." I rubbed the top of his dark buzz-cut hair and did my best to fake a calm as I frantically went to work setting his machine up.

He'd been on antibiotics all week, but the infection in his lungs wasn't budging this time. Months ago, Travis's nebulizer had been nothing more than an expensive paperweight that collected dust. But, over the last few weeks, it'd gotten so bad that we'd had to buy a spare to keep in his room.

I'd thought it was bad when he couldn't make it through the day without at least one breathing treatment, but now, we were up to three.

My son was eleven. He should have been out playing soccer and being a little shit, pulling pranks on the girls he liked—not waking up at three in the morning and struggling for survival. And, with every passing day, as he slipped further down the inevitable slope, I became more and more terrified that, one day, I'd lose him.

His lungs rattled as he sucked in so hard that the wheeze could have been heard throughout the house.

The familiar buzz filled the room as the nebulizer roared to life.

"Calm down, and try to breathe," I whispered, my heart shattering as I placed the mouthpiece between his lips, his pale, shaky hand coming up to hold it in place.

Jesus. This was a bad one.

I sank to the cold tile floor at his feet, my heart in my throat, and draped my arm over his thigh. My boy was a fighter, so I couldn't be sure if my presence helped him, but the contact did wonders for me.

I timed my breathing with his, and within minutes, I was lightheaded. I couldn't imagine how he was still upright.

*Please, God.* For as many times over the last three years that I'd bargained with the Lord in exchange for Travis's health, I should have been a priest.

A vise wrenched my chest. The breathing treatment wasn't helping. At least not fast enough.

A wave of dread rolled in my stomach. He was going to hate me. But I was the parent; it was my job to make the hard choices—even if they destroyed me. His pain and struggle coursed through my veins, too. This wasn't only his fight. It affected us all. If anything ever happened to him, I'd have to carry that hole in my soul for the rest of my life.

I'd promised him that I'd take care of him. I hadn't promised him that I'd be his friend while I did it. "Hannah, can you go grab Daddy's cell phone?"

"No!" Travis choked.

I closed my eyes and leaned my head against his shoulder. "Buddy, I'm sorry."

"I'm…not…going," he wheezed.

I swallowed hard to pack the overwhelming emotion down. I had to be strong enough for all of us—regardless that parts of my heart were crashing to the ground.

I couldn't go through this again.

But I couldn't *not* go through it again, either.

"You have to go, Trav."

On weak legs, he shot to his feet, but his balance was off and it sent him stumbling forward.

Lurching up, I caught him around the waist before he

cracked his head on the vanity. The nebulizer clattered against the floor and the buzzing droned on as he fought against me.

His movements were sluggish and his hands were slow, but for the way each blow slayed me, he might as well have been a championship boxer. God knew I'd welcome a TKO if it would soothe him.

"I'm sorry," I murmured, dragging him into my chest.

"I hate you," he cried, refusing to give up.

He didn't. Travis loved me. I knew that was as true as the sky was blue. But, if he needed an outlet for his anger, I'd be it every single time.

I gave him a gentle squeeze. "I'm so sorry."

He didn't hug me back, but I didn't need him to. I just needed him to keep breathing.

When Hannah reappeared with my phone, I guided Travis to sit on the toilet.

As expected, he was crying. I couldn't fault him. I wanted to fucking cry too.

It wasn't fair. None of it.

Lifting my phone to my ear, I hit send. As it rang, I bent, and scooped the plastic tubing up, and passed it back to my son. "Finish that and we'll head to the hospital."

He glared up at me, giving it the pre-teen attitude that seemed to be bred into kids, but he was too weak to properly snatch it from my hand.

A sleepy, "Hello?" came through the phone.

"Mom. Hey, can you meet me at the hospital to get Hannah?"

Her bed squeaked as she presumably climbed out of it. "How bad?"

I glanced at Travis, watching him sway with every breath. He refused me his gaze, but he was listening.

"Hannah, stay with your brother," I ordered, walking out of the bathroom.

I didn't answer her question until I was in my room. I went straight to my closet and changed into a shirt and jeans before slipping a pair of sneakers on.

"Pretty bad."

"Oh God," she whispered. "Yeah. Okay. I'm on my way. Hurry, but drive safe."

I then moved to my dresser to collect my wallet and my keys. Closing my eyes, I pinched the bridge of my nose. "Yeah. Same to you."

With a deep breath that I hoped would ease the hollow ache that never seemed to leave me anymore, I opened my eyes.

Catherine was staring back at me.

I wasn't positive why I left that picture on my dresser. I'd told myself that it was for the kids. So they could feel like she was still a part of our lives, despite the fact that it was now only the three of us.

I picked the picture up. She was smiling at the camera, her brown eyes glistening with unshed emotion, Travis wrapped in a swaddling blanket, mere hours old, tucked into the crook of her arm. I traced my fingers over the top of his dark, unruly hair as if I could comb it down, but my gaze drifted to his mother. It had only been three years since she'd died, but so much had changed.

She'd have known what to do with Travis. How to heal him. Maybe not physically, but emotionally. I remembered the first time he'd had an episode. I'd raced around the house, calling 911 frantic while she'd calmly sat next to him, rubbing his back and whispering reassuring words into the top of his hair. She was in agony, but she kept it together for him, a skill that had taken me over three years to master. She'd always been so good at reading his mood and rationalizing with him to take his medications. If he'd needed something, she had known instinctively. I'd often thought that watching the two of them together was one of the most beautiful things I'd ever seen.

She hadn't bumbled. Or faltered. She'd been a rock.

I wasn't like Catherine.

I was weak.

And exhausted.

And so damn scared.

But, even if it destroyed me, I would be there for him. That was one thing that would never change.

So, no. I wasn't like Catherine at all.

When I heard the nebulizer turn off, I set the picture back on the dresser and stared my wife straight in the eyes as I whispered, "I hate you so fucking much."

# TWO

## Charlotte

"I'll send her in right away, Mr. Clark," I said, backing out of the door, a wide smile stretching my lips.

It was fake—both the promise and the smile. I was exhausted. I'd been at the hospital for almost twenty-four hours, and sleeping stretched out between two rolling chairs had been exactly as restful as it sounded.

"Hey, Denise," I called, strolling over to the nurses' station, my tired feet screaming with every step. "Mr. Clark needs help to the bathroom."

She looked up from the computer screen with a scowl. "You have lost your damn mind."

I forced a grin, setting my clipboard on the desk and then flopping down into the chair beside her. Yawning, I pulled my disheveled hair into a ponytail.

I needed a haircut. Strike that. I needed a shower, a massage, a meal that was not prepared in the microwave, a week-long date with the backs of my eyelids, and *then* a haircut.

With my schedule, a unicorn sighting would have been more likely.

"Sorry," I mumbled around another yawn.

She rolled her eyes so hard that her retinas fully disappeared. "If I go back in that man's room, you're going to have to perform the surgical reattachment of his hand." She rocked back in her chair while crossing her arms over her chest. "I get it when the old-timers come in with dementia. They can't help themselves. But that man is forty and his only ailment is a nasty case of smokes-two-packs-a-day-induced asthma. Last I checked, your lungs *do not* affect your cognitive abilities." She paused and looked back at her computer, muttering, "Though the concussion I'm going to give that fool if he grabs my ass again will."

It sounded like a joke, so I offered her a chuckle, hoping that it came off as genuine.

Meanwhile, I stared at my watch.

*One hour.*

The minute hand had finally caught up with me.

When I'd gotten the call about Mr. Clark being admitted, a large part of me hoped I'd get tangled up and lose track of time.

But, regardless of how desperately I tried, I'd never be able to forget that day.

With nothing left to celebrate, that day only served as a reminder that I'd survived another year in the darkness he'd left behind.

"Look… I, um," I stalled. "I have to go. Can you *please*

make sure someone gets in there to help him?"

On a dramatic gasp, she clutched her chest. "Dear God, is the world ending?" She glanced around the nurses' station and asked everyone and no one, "Did Dr. Mills seriously just say she needed to go? It must be the rapture." Lifting her hands up to the heavens, she rejoiced, "Praise Jesus, I'm right with the Lord!"

"Ha. Ha," I deadpanned.

Okay. It could be said that I worked a lot. So much so that the running joke around the hospital was that I was a vampire who didn't require sleep to survive. For my last birthday, the residents had all chipped in and bought me a life-size Ian Somerhalder cardboard cutout. Apparently, he played a vampire in a TV show or something. But considering I didn't own a television, the humor was lost on me.

While my days were spent seeing patients at my office across town, my nights were all-too-often spent at the hospital. I was one of the few pulmonologists who came in any time a patient of mine was admitted. It wasn't that I didn't trust the on-call doctors—not exactly. They were talented. (Well, except Blighton. I wouldn't let that idiot treat my goldfish. And I didn't even have a goldfish.) My patients depended on me, and my peace of mind came with the knowledge that they were getting the best possible care I could offer them. If that meant I had to be available to them twenty-four-seven, so be it. Besides, it's not like I had much else going on in my life.

The most exciting thing that had happened to me outside of medicine in the last year was the blind date my best friend had guilted me into with the son of her hairdresser. His name was Hal, and he was an accountant. And not the sexy-nerdy type. I'm talking the balding, boring, pocket-protector-wearing kind. I'd sneaked out of the bathroom window halfway through dinner, and the following Monday, Rita had been forced to find someone new to touch up her roots. Luckily, she'd appeared to have learned her lesson and hadn't mentioned setting me up again.

I looked back at my watch.

*Fifty-nine minutes.*

After contemplating swinging through the infectious-disease lab to see if I could catch a dreaded—but curable—illness, I finally gave up and pushed to my feet. There was no way to avoid it. And the sooner I made an appearance, the sooner I could leave and put the entire day behind me for another year.

"I'll see you tomorrow, Denise."

Out of the corner of my eye, I caught her doing the sign of the cross as she called out, "Have a good one, Dr. Mills!"

As I waited for the elevator, nerves and dread brewed within me.

I could do this. It wasn't my first rodeo. I just had to show my face. Slap a smile on. Offer a few hugs. And then get the fuck out of there.

Oh, and be gutted all over again. Too easy.

I groaned as I punched the button for the parking garage.

"Charlotte, wait!" Greg yelled, attempting to slide inside the elevator with me. He managed to get his upper body through before the doors closed. "Shit!" he exclaimed as the elevator went into some kind of accordion mode, repeatedly opening and closing on him.

I could have helped by pressing the Open Door button, but I didn't. It was the most entertainment I was going to get all day.

Crossing my arms over my chest, I didn't try to hide my grin as he continued his battle with the elevator.

"What the hell?" he growled.

The doors finally gave up and his lanky body fell inside, banging into the wall.

I choked on a laugh and barely managed to get out, "Are you okay?"

"Seriously?" He snatched the lapels on his white coat back into place.

"You…uh"—I cleared the humor from my voice before finishing—"might want to report that to maintenance. Real safety hazard."

He narrowed his eyes, and it made my smile spread.

Nothing in this world gave me more pleasure than pissing off Greg Laughlin. It hadn't always been that way. Greg and I had been close since medical school. He was smart, handsome, and even funny in a weird way. If I'd had any interest in men whatsoever back then, I might have considered dating him. Fortunately, I'd dodged that bullet.

He'd married our mutual friend, now office manager, Rita, while we were still in our residencies. Greg and I both specialized in pulmonology, and the minute we'd been able, it was a no-brainer to go into private practice together. He was a good doctor but, as it turned out, absolute shit for a husband.

Earlier that week, I'd found out that he was sleeping with my head nurse. Talk about awkward. Rita was heartbroken, my nurse had quit, and my only way to exact any kind of revenge on my partner was through the karma-controlled doors of a malfunctioning elevator.

"I'm glad you enjoyed that," he snipped, finger-combing his thinning, brown hair.

"Oh, I truly did." I laughed.

"I've been texting you all day."

"I know. I've been *avoiding* you all day."

His lip curled in disbelief. "You can't avoid me."

"Um…I'm pretty sure I can. Remember, I've been doing it *all day*?"

The elevator came to a stop and I stepped off into the parking garage—not surprisingly, so did he.

"Is this about Rita?" he asked incredulously. "Still?"

I stopped and slowly turned to face him. "Uh…you cheated on my best friend. With my nurse. I'm pretty sure there is no statute of limitations on how long I'm allowed to be angry about that." I stabbed a finger in his direction. "*Especially* considering it's only been a week."

His head snapped back. "Jeez, you're cranky today."

I turned away and yelled, "Get used to it!" over my shoulder, my voice echoing off the concrete pillars.

"I wanted to make sure you'd be at the Fling this weekend."

I came to a screeching halt and whirled back around. "What?"

"The Fling," he clarified without actually clarifying anything.

"Yeah. I know what you said. But what do you mean *this weekend*?"

Every fucking year, Rita and Greg insisted on hosting this big Spring Fling for all of our patients and their families. It was a nice gesture, but Rita took it over the top. Face painting, bounce houses, carnival games.

Which meant: Kids. Kids. Kids.

Which meant: I avoided it at all costs.

"I...I thought that was at the end of the month?" I remembered because I'd specifically put in for a four-day vacation to ensure I wouldn't have to attend.

"No. We had to bump it up after the venue decided to schedule construction for that weekend. Last I heard, Rita was still scrambling to find a new caterer, but we at least have a new location."

I blinked, doing my best to keep my expression passive so as not to reveal the anxiety spiraling within me. "I can't make it."

"Oh, come on, Char. We've required the entire staff to be there. You can't skip out. They already call you the ice queen."

My back shot ramrod straight, and my mouth gaped. "They call me the ice queen?"

He rocked onto his toes then back onto his heels while ruefully scratching the back of his neck. "Actually, they call you worse, but ice queen is the only one of those nicknames I didn't start."

"What the hell, Greg!"

"Relax. It's just a little office humor."

I glared. "I'm their boss."

"Exactly. Which is why you need to be at the Fling." An arrogant smirk pulled at the corner of his lips. "Listen, just come for a little while. Make an appearance. Play nice with the patients and staff. And, if you so happen to find it in your new warm and loving, not at all icy, heart while you are there, I'd appreciate it if you could talk Rita into letting me come home."

My glare intensified. "Are you kidding me? I emailed her step-by-step instructions on how to castrate you last night."

He grinned. "You forget I was there to witness your surgical rotation. With your instruction, the worst she could do is give me a clean shave." He pointedly glanced at his zipper.

I lifted my hand to halt the conversation. "You know what? I'm done discussing your testicles. I have somewhere to be."

He arched an incredulous eyebrow. "Where the hell are you going? I didn't think you had patients on Wednesdays."

"I *do* have a life outside of work, you know."

"Psssh…sure." His mouth split into a wide, toothy grin, and he shoved his hands into the pockets of his coat. "Seriously though. Where ya headed?"

As mad as I was with Greg for being a philandering piece of shit who had hurt my girl and cost me a damn good nurse with slightly questionable morals, he was still my friend. And being the ice queen of North Point Pulmonology meant I didn't have many of those.

So I went with honesty.

"It's March seventh," I whispered.

"March sev—" He didn't finish before the light of understanding hit his eyes. "Oh God, Charlotte. I'm so sorry." His whole face softened, and he took a step toward me, the apology carved into his every feature. "I'm so sor—"

"It's okay," I said to let him off the hook. But it was yet another lie. Nothing was okay on March seventh. "I need to go before I'm late."

He nodded sheepishly. "Okay. Yeah. Go. Get out of here."

I stood for a few beats longer, waiting for an earthquake to hit. Or maybe a sinkhole to swallow the garage. But, when it never happened, I forced myself to my car.

And then, with an unwavering ache in my chest, I drove to my personal version of hell.

# THREE

## Porter

"NO. WAIT...I JUST..." WITH THE PHONE STILL PRESSED to my ear, I hung my head. "Yes, I'll hold."

God...would this day ever end?

After I'd spent a sleepless night with Travis at the hospital, I'd walked outside to discover a flat tire, which made me late to the walkthrough with the city inspector. And then he found four violations that my contractor swore weren't his fault. It was going to take at least a week to get everything up to code, including changes that would require removing one, if not both, of the freezers.

More time. More money. At that rate, it'd be a goddamn miracle if we opened on time.

It had been three years since my brother and I had gone into business together, but in that time, I'd completely forgotten what a nightmare it was to open a new restaurant. Though, that might be because, back then, I had been desperate for the distraction. Back then, I'd been floundering in virtually every aspect of life. I'd gone from being a workaholic investment banker to a single father of two literally overnight. Hannah was only six months old at the time, but Travis was eight. Watching my son nearly collapse from grief was more than I could bear. In the weeks that followed, he became angry and began lashing out at anyone and everyone he could reach. First and foremost: me. I couldn't blame him; I was pretty damn pissed at the universe too.

But he made me recognize that something had to change. I couldn't keep going to work, pulling sixty-hour weeks, and using nannies and babysitters to deal with the fallout Catherine had left behind.

In order for us to heal, we had to do it together.

I was all they had left.

*They* were all *I* had left.

Well, them and the acidic anger eating me away from the inside out.

I'd become a shell of the man who'd once smiled because it felt natural and laughed because everything held humor if you looked close enough.

That had all died with Catherine.

She'd ruined me.

And, worse, she'd ruined our children too.

The pain I'd felt when my son had looked up at me the day of his mother's funeral and asked, "Who's going to take care of me now?" had shattered me.

Hate and despair fused within me, plunging me into the darkness. I lost my job after I'd punched my boss when he'd dared to insinuate that I needed to take a few days off. And then it was just me and the kids functioning without feeling.

After Catherine, the world wasn't such a beautiful place anymore. It was sick and tainted, sucking the life out of me with every passing day.

Despite how isolating those first few months felt, I wasn't struggling alone. I had an amazing family who rallied around me and the kids.

Tanner was a lot of things: arrogant, obnoxious, irresponsible.

But he was also my little brother.

As a world-renowned chef, complete with his own show on The Food Channel, he stayed busier than I could ever imagine. But, when I found myself on my knees at the mercy of the universe, he stepped up in a big way.

He proposed that I partner with him to start a restaurant. As the head of the business side of the house, I would be allowed the freedom to make my own schedule and, if need be, bring the kids to work with me.

While it sounded like an appealing offer, I laughed at him. I could barely scramble eggs. What the hell did I know about starting a restaurant? But he assured me he knew what he was doing.

It was a huge fucking lie.

He'd vastly underestimated all the things that happened outside the kitchen.

Payroll? Staffing? Marketing? Customer service?

We were in way over our heads, but we were the Reese brothers, so we buckled down and forged ahead—fighting with each other every step of the way.

Christ, Tanner and I didn't agree on anything. That had

been the case for most of our lives, and I had no clue why we'd thought working together would be any different.

And, trust me, it wasn't.

During one of our early conversations, he'd specifically told me that he wanted something casual. To me, that meant burgers and fries he could spice up with some of his signature flares. So, one weekend, while he was gallivanting in New York, rubbing elbows with the likes of Bobby Flay and Wolfgang Puck, I did some preliminary planning. Hand on the Bible, I thought he was going to have a stroke when I showed him my Trapper Keeper (the only true way to organize). He balked at the location I'd picked, laughed at the proposed ambiance, and appeared downright offended by my suggested price point.

So we did what any two men in our early thirties would do to solve a disagreement. We built a Ninja Warrior course in the backyard and competed against each other, the victor earning the right to make the final decisions on everything from the menu to the table decor. I'd like to note that it was a hell of a lot safer than the bareknuckle cage match he'd first proposed.

Smiling, I was lost in fond memories of my come-from-behind victory the day we'd named the restaurant when my cell phone started ringing. Wedging the office phone between my shoulder and my ear, I began patting down the stacks of papers strewn haphazardly across my desk. A cup of pens fell off the side, scattering over the floor during my search, but I finally found my cell hiding between an empty to-go container and one of Hannah's Barbie dolls.

"Hello."

"Mr. Reese?"

"This is he."

"This is Harvey from Total Electric—"

Just then, I heard the same question in my other ear. "Mr. Reese?"

I pivoted the cell away from my mouth and spoke into the office line. "Yes! I'm here."

"Sorry about your wait. It'll be just a minute longer," she said.

My shoulders fell. I'd been on hold with the doctor's office so often over the last week that I'd memorized the majority of their mind-numbing hold music. Trust me, no one had the space in their brains to store the jazz instrumental versions of the Jackson Five. But, if I could get Travis an appointment with Dr. Mills, it could have become the soundtrack of my life, for all I cared.

"No problem," I replied with reluctance.

"Fantastic!" Harvey exclaimed. "We'll get this scheduled for next week."

I swung my cell back down to my mouth. "Wait. What the hell are you talking about?" I barked at Harvey.

"Excuse me?" the woman in my other ear said.

"Not you," I snapped only to remember I was supposed to be in ass-kiss mode. "I mean…I'm sorry. I was talking to someone else."

"Right," she drawled, but a second later, a saxophone flared on the hook of "I Want You Back."

I shifted the phones again so only Harvey could hear me (hopefully). "What the hell do you mean, *next week*?"

"As I said…we've had a slight delay—"

Clearly, the day *could* get shittier.

"Listen, pal, I don't care if you have to drive to the factory and assemble the damn things yourself. We went with your bid even though your prices were astronomical because you promised you could deliver on schedule."

"Yes. But things have changed."

"Then un-fucking-change them!"

His voice became cautious. Wisely so. "I can get you six tomorrow and the rest by the first of next week."

"Our soft opening is next week." I rocked back in my chair, but I wasn't calm in the least. Without those lights, we were fucked. "Listen, *Harvey.*" I stressed his name to be a dick. "This might be a stretch, but I'm thinking people are going to want to *see* their food before they eat it, and it's my job to make sure that happens. So hear me when I say this: I want them *all* today or keep the damn things. Central Electric has what we need." They didn't. "In stock." Seriously, I was so full of bullshit. "I'm done waiting."

"But—"

"But nothing! You're wasting my fucking time. Either get me the lights or get off my fucking line so I can call Central Electric." *Please, God, do not get off my line.*

He went quiet, and I waited anxiously.

"What about tomorrow?" he asked.

I launched to my feet, quietly celebrating as much as I could with two phones held to my ears. When I got myself back together, I cleared my throat and said, "I'm not happy about this. But you come through tomorrow and we won't completely write off doing future business with you again."

"We'd appreciate that," he said evenly, probably doing some silent celebrating of his own. (Or, at least, I pretended as much.)

"Hi, Mr. Reese. This is Rita Laughlin," the woman on the other phone said.

Without saying goodbye to Harvey, I hung up.

"Riiiitttta," I purred. "You are a hard woman to reach. Please, just call me Porter."

"Sorry about that. I've been slammed this week. I'm planning this Spring Fling and…" She paused. "Sorry. I'm rambling. What can I do for you, Porter?"

First name. I was *so* in there.

"I need an appointment with Dr. Mills."

"Oh," she said, sounding surprised. "Our receptionist should have been able to handle that for you."

I drew in a deep breath and finished with, "For my son."

"Ohhhh," she drawled in understanding. "I'm sorry. Dr. Mills doesn't—"

"Treat children. Yes. So I've been told. But I'm asking *you*. To ask him—"

"Her," she corrected.

"Right. Her. Sorry. All I'm asking is for you to ask her to make an exception. Just once."

She sucked in a sharp, hissing breath. "I'm sorry. She doesn't make exceptions. Though I have the name of a fantastic pediatric pulmonologist—"

"Martin, Craig, Lorenz, Rogers, McIssanson, Goldmen," I listed. "We've seen them *all*. And each one has assured me that Mills is the best."

"I'm sorry, Mr. Reese."

Shit, back to my last name. I was losing traction.

Gentling my voice, I turned the charm on. "What if you

schedule *me* a consult and I'll ask her myself? Could you be a dear and do that for me?"

"No. I can't be *a dear* and do that for you," she clipped.

Okay. Too much charm. Time to reel it back in.

"Perhaps I could make a monetary donation." I had plenty of money. Plenty meaning I could afford private tutors, nice daycares, and impromptu family vacations. Though constructing a hospital wing in Dr. Mills's honor was pretty much off the table. Unless they accepted a payment plan—for individual bricks.

"We don't accept bribery, either," she said dryly. "Look, Dr. Laughlin is Dr. Mills's partner. He has a few openings. I could probably get your son on his schedule."

"Ugh." I groaned. "I've heard terrible things about him."

She didn't immediately reply, and it took several seconds for the memory of her last name to hit me.

I pinched the bridge of my nose and mouthed a string of expletives to myself. "I mean…I'm sure he's an amazing—"

"No, you were pretty much spot-on the first time. He's my soon-to-be ex-husband."

A blast of relief surged through me. "I'm sorry to hear that."

"Listen, I really want the best for your son. But I've known Dr. Mills for a lot of years. And she does *not* treat children. No exceptions. Now, if you'll excuse me. I have—"

My stomach dropped. "Please don't hang up," I rushed out, my anxiety climbing. "We've done the breathing treatments and inhalers. But nothing seems to keep him out of the hospital anymore. He's getting weaker, and the other pulmonologists expect us to accept that this is how things are going to be for him. But I'm not quitting on my son. I *need* Dr. Mills. Please. He's eleven, but he's never been able to be a kid. Help me give him that."

"Porter," she sighed.

Back to first names.

"Rita, all I'm asking is that you let me talk to her. I'll do anything."

"Anything. Right."

But I'd never been more serious in my life. I was sick and tired of watching my son waste away. I *needed* that appointment.

"You like steak, Rita?"

"Uhh…."

I blew out a hard breath and grasped at the only card I had up my sleeve—a silly two of clubs. "I own a restaurant. You get me in with Dr. Mills and I'll get you free steaks for life."

I expected her to laugh. Maybe even hang up and block my number.

But I'd never expected the pique of interest in her voice as she replied, "You own a *restaurant*?"

# FOUR

## Charlotte

"HAPPY BIRTHDAY, LUCAS," I WHISPERED, STARING UP AT his picture on Brady's mantel.

My heart ached no less than it had the first minute I'd realized he was gone. And on every single one of the 3,467 days since. It had been almost ten years since I'd seen my son, and the wounds were no closer to being healed. Time wasn't the miracle cure so many had told me it would be. For me, time wasn't even a Band-Aid.

Reality slashed me every morning when I opened my eyes. Though, through the years, I'd become too callused and numb to feel it anymore. The constant agony had become a way of life.

I stayed busy, kept to myself, and made a difference in other people's lives as some sort of penance for having failed the one person who had truly depended on me.

That same act of voluntary self-punishment was exactly

how I ended up at Brady's house once a year. With Lucas gone, we had nothing tying us together. No forced relationship God knew neither of us wanted to maintain. Yet there I stood, staring up at a framed picture of my newborn little boy on what would have been his tenth birthday.

"You coming outside?" Tom asked gently.

Wearing a weak smile, I turned to face him.

As we all had, he'd aged. But he'd done it well. The pepper was now missing from his silver hair, and the tiny crinkles that had once pinched around his eyes when he smiled were now a permanent fixture regardless of his expression. He was a far cry from the man who'd knelt in front of me that day at the park, swearing to me that he would never stop trying to find my son.

It was funny. Looking back, I'd realized that not once had he told me that he *would* find him. Just that he would never stop trying. Fortuitous as it might have been.

"I'd rather be shot," I replied softly.

After brushing his sports coat back, he slid his hands into the pockets on his khaki slacks. "That makes two of us, then."

I went back to staring at the picture. It was the same one on my nightstand. I'd long since memorized every curve of his cherubic face. Yet, somehow, seeing it in Brady's house and not stained with my tears made it feel new.

"Your mom just got here. You've got about ninety seconds before she comes looking for you."

My lids fluttered closed as I sighed. "Christ. Why do they insist on doing this every year?"

His footsteps moved closer, and his hand landed on my shoulder. "It's therapeutic, Charlotte."

I shook my head, knotting my hands in front of me. "No. It's torture. And, quite honestly, it's a tad disturbing."

"Yeah, okay. It's a little bit of that, too." His hand squeezed gently. "But it makes your mom smile, and Brady usually manages to pull his head out of his ass for at least thirty minutes."

My shoulders shook as a sad laugh escaped my lips.

Tom Stafford was the father I'd never wanted. He was such an amazing man, but I wished with my whole heart that we'd never been forced to meet. But I guessed, if there were any silver lining to be found in this whole traumatic experience, he would be it.

He'd been the detective in charge of Lucas's disappearance since day one. In the beginning, we'd spoken every day—usually multiple times. But, as time had marched on, leads becoming fleeting and hope fading out of reach, our relationship had become personal. Whether it was Saturday-night dinners, the occasional drink, or his silence on the other end of the line when I'd call him at three a.m. to sob, he was always there. While I'd never specifically asked why he was so good to me, he'd told me years earlier that he'd lost his daughter to an accidental drowning when she was three. I figured I must have reminded him of her. I don't know how I would have made it through those first pitch-black years without him.

"You going to ask her out today?" I asked.

His hand spasmed. "Leave it alone."

"It's been five years since Dad died," I stated, peering up at him over my shoulder.

His hazel eyes turned dark as he stared down at me. "I know. I was at the funeral, Charlotte."

"Then you know it's time for her to move on. She's lonely, Tom."

"Yeah. I know that too. Actually, it's time for *both* of the stubborn-ass Mills women to move on," he said pointedly.

I rolled my eyes and stepped away. I wasn't a nun or anything, but when the highlights of your social life revolved around dinner and drinks with a fifty-six-year-old man who was sweet on your mother, it could be said that you weren't exactly far from it.

"Billy was asking about you again. I could—"

"No way," I said, cutting him off. "We are *not* discussing Billy Weiner again."

His lips twitched with amusement. "Come on. He's a good guy. I'd marry you off to him if I could."

"His last name is Weiner."

A smile broke across his face. "Give him a shot, sweetheart. Things work out, you can make him take your last name at the wedding."

I almost smiled. For the briefest of seconds, the guilt I carried around like a boulder in my chest seemed to defy gravity.

Almost.

Until it came crashing down at the sound of his voice.

"We're about to do cake," Brady announced from the doorway. "You coming outside?"

Tom went on alert as we both spun to face Lucas's father.

I'd known that today was going to be hard. Every year, I'd dreaded that party like the plague. But this year was different, and I'd been preparing myself more than usual.

His name was William Lucas Boyd. My mother had informed me the day he was born. But the sight of him felt like

I'd been hit by a freight train.

My heart ached.

My hands twitched.

My mind screamed.

My conscience wept.

The sight of Brady holding a six-month-old little boy with black hair and brown eyes was worse than any slice from the blade of reality. It was a direct hit from the rusty, jagged knife of the past.

My back collided with Tom's hard chest as I blinked frantically, trying to stay in the present. Memories of Brady holding Lucas flooded my brain until I was choking on them.

The chill of Brady's gaze raked over me as he shifted the baby in his arms. "Jesus, Charlotte. You couldn't take the day off?"

"I..." I smoothed the top of my scrubs down and did the best I could to keep my voice even. "I had a patient. I just came from the hospital."

"Well, I'm so glad you could find the time in your busy schedule to join us."

It could have been an innocent statement coming from anyone else. But not from Brady.

It still killed me the way he so fiercely blamed me for everything. It'd been almost ten years and the ever-present disdain still radiated from his eyes when we saw each other. I'd often thought I could have waited a hundred years and he still would have scowled at me from the grave.

Time hadn't healed his wounds, either.

He hated me. I could have lived with that if he hadn't been the only piece of Lucas I had left.

And I'd lost that too.

It was no secret that I hadn't handled the emotional upheaval of Lucas's disappearance well. Brady had lost his mind when I'd gone back to school five days after our son was taken. But everyone had their own ways of dealing with hardship—or, in our case, life-altering devastation. For me, it was to throw myself into my career.

I couldn't sit at home, waiting for the phone to ring or a knock at the door from someone saying that they had found him. The what-ifs and regrets of that day were nearly crippling without being forced to relive them for hours on end. Yes, I waited with bated breath for someone to bring him back to me. Praying to any and every god who would ever exist. Crying oceans of tears. Losing parts of myself in the depths of despair. But, no matter how many times I'd bargained with the universe, nothing had changed. I wanted my son back more than I wanted to see another sunrise, but with no leads, there was only so much I could do.

Brady took to the media and worked closely with the Center for Missing and Exploited Children while I desperately tried to disappear into the shadows. Our story had made national news for a brief spell. And the finger-pointing had been more than I could handle.

*What kind of a mother leaves their child alone in a stroller?*

*She deserves to be in jail.*

*She probably killed him and made up this whole kidnapping thing as a cover.*

Those were a few of the most popular comments echoing through the media.

By way of the popular opinion, I was guilty.

I was barely surviving my own condemnation without the entire world casting stones at me too.

So I went back to work, doing everything possible to keep myself from self-destructing. And people misunderstood this as me being unaffected. I'd sacrificed everything for my career. Love. Friends. Time with my family. But make no mistake about it. Without hesitation, I would have given it all up for one second with Lucas.

Straightening my backbone, I refused to show Brady any weakness. My heart was breaking, but I wouldn't allow him to make that day any more difficult than it already was. "I'm here, okay? Let's cut the bullshit. Have some cake. And then go back to pretending the other doesn't exist."

His jaw ticked as he stared down at me. "Right. Of course. Pretending. The Charlotte Mills way."

I barked a humorless laugh. "Yeah, Brady. I'm the one pretending as you sing 'Happy Birthday' to our ten-year-old *missing* child."

The words hadn't escaped my mouth before I regretted them. It was a stupid jab spoken out of anger. I should have known better than to provoke him. I'd become skilled at dodging his insults over the years, but that one statement opened me up for Brady's signature blow. There wasn't armor in the world strong enough to protect me from its assault.

I braced.

His face became hard, and his nostrils flared with rage.

It was coming.

The air around us chilled.

"Brady," Tom warned at my back.

But it was too late…

"And whose fault is that, Charlotte?"

The *words* tore through me. It was a truth and a fact not even I could deny.

*Mine.*

It was my fault.

Always and forever.

"Enough!" Her voice breezed into the silent room like the warning whistle of an arrow.

I imagined her walking in like a superhero, her arm stretched out in front of her, the furniture sliding back to the walls at her will. In truth, she tiptoed in on a pair of kitten heels, wearing a pair of crisp, white linen pants and a bright-coral silk blouse that popped in contrast to her dark brown bob. At fifty-eight, she was just as beautiful as she'd been when I was a kid. But, for as petite and proper as she appeared to be on the outside, on the inside, my mother was a warrior. She'd fought the entire world on my behalf when Lucas had gone missing.

"Susan..." Brady started, but he didn't bother finishing the thought. He was no opponent for the likes of Susan Mills. Not many people were.

"Today is not about you, Brady," she snapped. "You stand there, holding your son, spewing insults and blame? It's never too early to teach your children a thing or two about understanding and forgiveness. Be an example for him." She palmed each side of William's tiny head, covering his ears, and then hissed, "And stop being an asshole on my grandson's birthday."

God, I loved my mom.

Brady shifted the baby in his arms, and without another word or glance in my direction, he backed out of the room, his tail firmly tucked between his legs.

My shoulders rounded forward as relief washed over me.

At five-six, I was over four inches taller than my mother, but when she wrapped me in her arms, I felt like a child again.

"Hey, love," she cooed, all signs of her hard-ass attitude erased.

"Hey, Mom," I murmured.

Tom ambled away, giving us space without wandering far.

"You okay?" she asked, stepping out of my embrace.

"I'm fine."

She kept her hands on my biceps and studied my face for any sign of a lie.

If she found any, she had the graciousness to let it go.

I wasn't fine. And I hadn't been in a long time. She'd hated it, but over the years, she'd had no choice but to accept it. The happy and carefree Charlotte Mills she'd raised had died on that fated September morning.

She slid her assessing gaze to the side. "You know, Tom. You *do* carry a gun. It wouldn't have killed you to take care of that situation before I got here."

He lifted his head from his phone, a small—and entirely handsome—smile pulling at his lips. "Not fond of spending my retirement in the slammer, Susan."

She grinned and then batted her eyelashes. (Legit Betty Boop–style.) "No. I guess we can't have that, now can we?"

I flicked my eyes between the two of them as they stood there staring at each other, the blatant chemistry damn near suffocating me.

God. I wanted that. With someone. Anyone. Though that would have probably required me to let someone in and allow them to get to know me. In a lot of ways, that insurmountable task seemed harder than finding out who had taken my son.

"Anyway," I drawled to break their invisible current.

Mom shook her head to snap herself out of it. "I hear it's time for cake."

My shoulders tensed. When would it stop hurting so damn much? I read in a book about grief once that it was all about baby steps, focusing on each individual day. It had been ten years and I still felt like I was living frozen in time, not necessarily waiting for him to come home but still unable to figure out how to move forward.

Maybe it was time for big steps. Giant, even. I couldn't keep doing this to myself. One day, I was going to wake up and realize that, in my desperate escape from the pain in the present, I'd let the future pass me by.

Hell, I'd already allowed a decade to slide into past tense.

What if I never got to meet someone who loved me the way my dad had loved my mom?

Or even experience the way Tom looked at her as though she were the only woman he'd ever seen?

If I kept on the same path, taking baby step after baby step, working myself to the bone to avoid reality, I was going to die on that path—miserable and alone.

But how do you move forward when all you really want is to go back?

"Charlotte," Mom prompted. "It's time."

She'd never been more right.

Sucking in a deep breath, I linked my arm with my mom's and then looked back at Lucas's picture above the fireplace. "Happy Birthday, baby."

And then, together, the three of us walked outside to have cake.

Tom stood at my side, doing his best to deflect Brady's glares, and my mom held my hand as I sobbed while singing the saddest rendition of "Happy Birthday" to ever be sung. Less than an hour later, I excused myself and headed home, where the pity party was just getting started.

# FIVE

## Porter

"UHHH OHHH," TANNER DRAWLED BEHIND A POT OF bubbling red sauce, a giant shit-eating grin pulling at his lips. "I spilled it on my shirt."

Gripping the back of my neck, I made a U-turn and continued to pace a path behind the row of cameramen and sound engineers.

Quietly, I mumbled to myself, "You always spill it on your shirt, asshole. Learn to lift a damn spoon to your mouth."

The idea of watching Tanner flirt with a camera while making vongoli was very low on my day's priority list. It was only slightly above being waterboarded and hung by my toenails. Sure, the day had been shitty, but that was pretty much the permanent order of my priority list when it came to watching my brother strip his shirt off for his adoring fans.

Yes. He was a chef. Not the star of *Magic Mike*, though if you asked the president at The Food Channel, the ratings were surprisingly similar.

"And cut!" the director yelled before turning a seriously scary glower my way. "You have got to stop talking!"

"I didn't say anything!" I defended—and lied.

I'd been grumbling under my breath for at least a half hour. She'd already threatened to throw me off the set once. But, really, the first time had been totally warranted. I wasn't a TV director and I knew beyond nothing about cooking, but even I could tell that he was stirring an empty pot.

"I can hear you! We can *all* hear you." She waved her arms around my brother's kitchen, motioning to a team of cameramen nodding in agreement.

Defiantly crossing my arms over my chest, I feigned ignorance. "Sorry. I don't know what you're talking about. Must have been someone else."

Her eyes bulged and her lips started doing this crazy twitching thing that made it look like she was having a seizure.

"Okay, okay," Tanner interjected, peeling the half apron from around his hips. "Andrea, can you give us a minute?"

She sliced her gaze over to me, but her words were aimed at my brother. "Absolutely, as long as you promise to get rid of him when you're done."

"Get rid of me? Are you kidding?" I stabbed a finger toward Tanner then hooked my thumb at my chest. "We share strands of the same DNA. And you want him to—"

Tanner gave my shoulder a hard shove before stating, "I'll get rid of him."

"The hell you will!" I shot back, but only because I was pissed. I wanted to leave more than she wanted me gone.

Shaking his head, he dug a pack of cigarettes from his

pocket and led me out to the porch. "Let's go. Spit it out. I've only got a minute to sort your shit, so talk fast."

"She's a witch," I grumbled, jutting my chin at the woman barking orders to someone on the other side of the sliding glass doors.

After flicking his lighter to life, he hovered the orange flame over the tip of the cigarette dangling between his lips and talked around it. "Amazing director, decent in bed, but crazier than a tiger on acid. I suggest you don't piss her off any more than you already have."

Raking a hand through my thick, blond hair, I asked in all seriousness, "Should I be concerned that you've seen a tiger on acid?"

He chuckled. "Probably. But let's deal with your shit first. Tell me what's got you ranting and pacing around like Dad the day we accidentally scratched his Vette?"

I scoffed. "Please. I'm nothing like Dad."

His baby-blue eyes, which matched my own, danced with humor. "That's probably because you'd never have the balls to buy a Vette. A ding on the ol' Tahoe just isn't the same." He grinned and exhaled a thick cloud of smoke through his nose.

I waved the smoke away from my face. "You're a dick. But I need a favor."

His smile grew. "Reeeeaaaallly?"

I mentally groaned. I hated asking him for shit. It was always the same song and dance, but as much as I would have liked to handle this thing with Dr. Mills on my own, I needed Tanner.

"What are you doing on Saturday?"

He tipped his head to the side and eyed me warily.

"Probably not whatever you're about to ask me to do."

"I need you to cook."

I'd spent the morning ordering a gazillion pounds of meat (rough exaggeration) and calling in four of our sous chefs to make burger patties, pasta salads, potato salads, and a bunch of other *amazing* picnic-style foods Tanner would *never* allow us to serve at the restaurant.

"You *need* me to cook for you every day. Seriously, I can't watch you make a PB and J without cringing, but why specifically on Saturday?"

"I'm trying to get Travis an appointment with that new pulmonologist, so I volunteered to cater their Spring Fling."

"And you think having celebrity chef Tanner Reese show up is going to help get your foot in the door?"

I rolled my eyes. "Your humility is astounding. No. I don't need *celebrity* Tanner Reese to do anything. I do, however, need my brother to show up, be charming, and grill a literal shit-ton of hamburgers. Though, if someone asks for an autograph, sign it. Just, please, for the love of all that's holy, *wait* for them to actually ask. It's embarrassing watching you snatch cocktail napkins out of people's hands each time you exit the kitchen. You have no idea how many of those 'collector's items' the bar staff throws away each night."

It was his turn to roll his eyes. "One time. *One* time." He paused and gazed off into the distance at the picturesque pond dancing in the background.

I'd always loved that plantation house, with its wraparound porches, oak-lined driveway, and the massive weeping willow that decorated the front lawn. It was the perfect house to raise a family. Thus, it had boggled my mind when my brother of all people had bought it two years earlier.

"No," he said absently.

"No, what?"

He turned to face me. "No, I'm not spending my first day off in almost a month making a bunch of burgers for a Spring Fling. Get Raul to do it."

I took a long stride toward him. "Don't fucking do the diva bit today."

He smiled. "I'm not being a diva. I'm exhausted. I need a day off."

"So take next weekend off," I offered—though I had no idea what the hell I'd do without him.

We booked out months in advance on the weekends. And, as much as I hated to admit it, most of that hype was because customers knew that Tanner would be there, not only in the kitchen, but also meandering around the dining room. Worse, with the soft opening of the new restaurant quickly approaching too, I doubted either one of us would be able to take a weekend off for a long while.

"Can't," he replied. "We have the Leblanc wedding reception. He paid a small fortune to buy us out for the night."

I ground my teeth, desperation getting the best of me. "I *need* you there." And then the truth escaped my mouth before I had a chance to stop it. "You have to come. What if she tells me no?"

He paused with the cigarette halfway to his mouth. "She?"

I interlocked my fingers and rested them on the top of my head. "Dr. Mills. I was kinda hoping you'd come and put her in that weird trance thing that makes women actually like you."

"The trance thing," he repeated, humor thick in his voice.

"I don't know. Okay? I just can't afford to fuck this up and I thought maybe, if you were there, I'd have a better shot at getting her to say yes."

I had no idea that a human face was capable of stretching that wide.

"Say it… You want celebrity Tanner Reese."

"No, what I want is for you to stop talking in third person."

"Say it."

"No."

"Then no. I can't make it."

"Fuck!" I exploded, tugging at the top of my hair. "Fine. I want the minor celebrity—"

"Major," he countered.

I glowered and then amended through clenched teeth, "*Major* celebrity Tanner to come—"

"Full name or it doesn't count."

Closing my eyes, I tipped my head back and stared up at the wooden slats of the second-floor balcony. "I need you, major celebrity Tanner Reese, to come cook burgers and help me schmooze a doctor into taking your nephew on as a patient."

When he didn't reply with a smartass comment, I pried my eyes open and found him watching me with a satisfied grin.

He smacked my arm before giving it a reassuring squeeze. "I'm fucking with you. I was in the minute you said it was for Trav."

I shrugged his hand off. "You're a dick." But knowing he'd be there lifted the weight of the world off my shoulders. If anyone could talk a middle-aged, crotchety doctor into treating Travis, it was my brother.

Laughing, he put his cigarette out and headed to the door. "Whatever you need, man. Text me the details and let yourself out." Just before the door closed behind him, he leaned his upper body out and said, "Go around the side of the house. I hear it's past Andrea's feeding time, and I don't have time to save your ass with the ladies twice in one week." He winked, and then he was gone.

He was seriously obnoxious, but with a barbeque to coordinate, a restaurant to open, two kids to pick up from my parents, an ambush medical consult to plan, and a beer calling my name from my refrigerator at home, I left his house smiling for the first time all day.

# SIX

## Charlotte

SOMETHING WAS WRONG WITH ME. AND MORE THAN THE normal bullshit that was always wrong with me. Usually by March ninth, I was done with the wallowing and I'd gotten my shit together. But it was now the tenth and I couldn't seem to emerge from the madness churning in my head. I wasn't sure if it was the realization that I'd had watching Tom fawn over my mom or maybe seeing Brady moving on with his new wife and son. Or maybe I'd finally gotten so lost in the darkness that I couldn't find my way out.

But, whatever it was, it was drowning me.

Mr. Clark had still been at the hospital, but I hadn't been able to drag myself up there to check on him. Instead, I'd allowed the on-call to treat him while I had lain in bed, soaking my pillow in salty tears, mourning the loss of what felt like my entire life.

It had been ten goddamn years; it should have been

getting easier to climb out of bed every morning, not harder. Yet, that morning, as I'd forced myself to get dressed and leave the house, it had seemed more difficult than ever.

Enough was enough. I couldn't keep living like that. That is if you could consider what I was doing *living* at all.

I needed something to change.

Anything.

Hell, maybe everything.

Deep down, I knew the truth. *I* was what needed to change. But it wasn't going to happen without conscious and *continuous* effort on my part. It was only that realization that had led me to attend the office Spring Fling.

"You came!" Rita exclaimed as I'd strolled up to the welcome table. She raked her gaze over me. "And…in a hoodie. How charming."

"Sorry. I didn't know cocktail attire was required."

I'd spent most of my free time mastering the skill of avoiding social gatherings. Baby showers. Birthdays. Weddings. Whatever. For a woman with three friends, I got invited to more shit than you could imagine. I'd found that, if I bought a gift card and sent it with my regrets, no one got pissy when I didn't show. Unfortunately, I didn't think it was financially responsible to mail a gift card to all thirty of the employees at our office with a note that said: *Yes. You were right. I am an ice queen and would rather eat hissing cockroaches than attend a damn carnival. Here, accept this fifty-dollar Walmart gift card in my absence.*

Though, judging by the side-eyes I'd received as I'd walked up, it probably would have been a welcome substitution.

"Why is everyone staring at me?" I whispered to Rita.

Folding her arms on top of the table, she leaned toward me and whispered back, "Because vampires can't walk in the sun, honey." She laughed. "I, for one, am thrilled you decided to come."

"I'm sure you are. It saves you the trouble of burning my house down like you threatened on my voicemail *twice* yesterday."

She beamed. "Yes. And that."

Rita was crazy. All hell on wheels, beauty queen wrapped in pearls and Southern charm. She'd threatened me with worse than burning my house down over the years. Honestly, I'd been a little disappointed with her creativity with that one.

She lifted a long strip of blue tickets into the air, her short, blond hair bouncing as she energetically explained, "Everything from lunch to face painting is one ticket. You get ten free. After that, you can purchase more right here with me. All monies collected go toward—"

"Where's Greg?" I asked, cutting her off. That speech was going to last for ten minutes, and she wasn't going to take a breath the entire time.

She frowned, her excitement about whatever charity she'd chosen to donate to this year disappearing at the mention of his name. "*Dr. Laughlin* is spending the day in the dunking booth."

I tsked in disappointment. "I thought we discussed the human dartboard?"

"I decided it might be a tad too violent for the kids."

"Yeah, but the dunking booth isn't nearly as satisfying to watch."

"I don't know about that." She leaned in close, partitioning off her mouth from the people around us and whispered, "I filled the tank with ice water and paid the pitchers from the local high school baseball team to rotate through the line for a few hours."

"Niiiiice," I praised.

Her red-painted lips split with pride. "If he's going to fire me, I'm going to earn it."

My head snapped back. "What are you talking about? He's not going to fire you."

"Oh please. How long do you think he's going to keep his ex-wife employed after I take him to the cleaners in divorce court?"

"I don't care what happens between you two. He's *not* firing you."

She reached across the table and squeezed my arm. "You're sweet, honey. But it's bound to happen. And I'll be honest, I'm not sure I can spend my days watching him parade around with whatever nurse he's got his eye on next."

I scoffed. "There isn't a woman in that office who would touch him with a ten-foot pole after the shit he and Tammy pulled on you. Besides, that office is half mine. You aren't going anywhere."

Her faced warmed and saddened at the same time. "And I appreciate that, but, Charlotte, it's time for me to move on. A man you love treats you like that, you don't sit around pining after him. You put on your tightest little black dress and your best pair of heels, and *strut* into the future." Her voice caught, but she kept right on smiling. "Life sucks sometimes. You and I know that better than anyone else, but we only get one."

I felt every single *word* slash through me.

I loved Rita. And, thanks to a bottle of tequila on Lucas's fourth birthday, she and Greg knew all about my situation. But my affections for her didn't stop the familiar resentment from roaring to life within me.

It happened when people tried to sympathize with me, comparing whatever sucky situation was plaguing their lives at the moment to the utter devastation that had destroyed mine. Sure, they were usually well meaning, but the words felt like a low blow, trivializing everything I'd experienced. Even coming from someone as kind as Rita, it felt like an insult.

She was losing her husband. I'm sure her heart was breaking, but it was still beating. It hadn't been ripped from her chest. Hope wouldn't become her greatest enemy, nor would guilt be her only company. Her days might be gray, but they wouldn't be midnight, every sunrise darker than the last. She had no comparison to the hell that was my life. I hated that Greg had turned out to be such a dick. It had pained me for her when the truth had come out.

But it wasn't the end for her.

One day, she'd get over him and start her life again. She'd smile and laugh and realize that it had all been for the best. She'd find someone better and start a family, thanking her lucky stars that he'd let her go so she could bask in the sunlight of her new life.

Meanwhile, I'd still be frozen in time, holding my breath for a future that would never come.

Unless...I could figure out how to change.

Swallowing hard, I faked a smile and tried to keep the cyclone of pain hidden.

"Enough heavy for one day," I urged quietly.

"Yes. Yes. You're right." She sniffled and swiped under her eyes, though no tears had escaped. "Go on. Get out of here and have some fun."

*Like that's going to happen.*

Lifting my tickets, I pointedly shook my them at her and made my escape.

"Oh, wait, Char!" she called.

Reapplying my mask, I turned back to face her. "What's up?"

"Do me a favor and take this over to the guy at the grill?" She thrust an empty pickle jar in my direction. "He needs a way to collect the tickets for lunch." She smiled—like, huge.

So huge that I went on alert. "Why are you looking at me like that?"

"Like what?" she said innocently, but that fucking smile stretched even wider.

I swirled my finger in the air to indicate her face. "Like *that*."

She shrugged. "I don't know what you're talking about?"

Swear to God.

Her.

Smile.

Grew.

Suspiciously, I glanced over my shoulder at a large, white tent positioned next to a grill with a pluming cloud of smoke floating out of it. There was a tall man with unruly, blond hair sticking out in all directions. The cause was clear as he fisted the top of it in frustration. He was wearing a pair of jeans and a white apron that had large, black handprints smudged across the front. His mouth moved a mile a minute as he scraped whatever he was massacring into a cardboard box at his feet.

Rita pressed the jar into my hand. "You should go talk to him."

I *should* have gone and rescued what I feared was going to be lunch from its fiery death. Instead, I continued watching him with curiosity as he slapped another round of raw burgers down, sparks shooting up around them.

"What the hell is he doing?" I asked.

"I don't know. Go ask him." She nudged my shoulder.

Understanding dawned on me and I swung my gaze to her. "Are you trying to set me up with that guy?"

"Dear God, no." She slapped a hand over her heart. "I'm about to reenter the dating world for the first time in eight years. I can't afford to risk that you'll praying-mantis a hot one like that." She shoved me forward. "Stop being so damn suspicious. He looks like he could use some help, and I'm smart enough to know that you're about to find somewhere to hide for the next hour until you can leave. So do us all a favor and do it"—she pointed a perfectly French manicured nail at the man—"over there."

I opened my mouth to defend myself, but she had been pretty much spot-on, so I quickly closed it.

"Go make sure there will be *edible* food to serve people and then you have my full permission to leave in two hours."

"One hour," I countered.

"One and a half."

"One hour, Rita. I need to get up to the hospital." Totally the truth. Mr. Clark was raising hell, and the nurses had been blowing my phone up while waiting for a discharge order.

"One hour and fifteen minutes," she bargained.

I extended a hand toward her. “One hour and I’ll pay to keep the baseball team until five.”

Her eyebrows shot up and her hand landed in mine so fast that I almost laughed.

“Deal.”

# SEVEN

## Porter

"SON OF A..." I TRAILED OFF BEFORE I HAD THE CHANCE to scandalize the ears of any children nearby. "Sorry, Porter. I can't make it. Angie *needs* me. You at least know how to grill, right?" I mocked my brother's voice while scraping another burnt burger off the fire and into the hidden bin at my feet, where at least ten others were in similar condition.

No. The answer was no. I didn't know how to grill—at least, not effectively. I must have missed that day in Manliness 101. But did I tell Tanner that? Fuck no. My brother was a jackass. He'd bailed on me only fifteen minutes before we were supposed to start because the woman he had been dating for approximately seven seconds needed him for moral support because her dog had died. I was a dog lover as much as the next guy, but come on. He'd known how much I was depending on him.

Then, in another show of astounding maturity, he'd hung up on me and turned his phone off.

I plopped another hand-molded patty on the grill. Using the long, metal spatula, I pointed at it and ordered in a low voice, "Don't fucking burn."

It was safe to say that I was seriously stressing out. Burning over a hundred burgers was hardly going to carry me into the good graces of the ageist Dr. Mills. But, just that morning, I'd held Travis as he'd struggled through yet another worthless breathing treatment. Something had to give.

Turning my attention away from the sizzling grill, I scanned the crowd. Children ran rampant through the grassy park, weaving between games and refreshment stands. That should have been Travis. Instead, he was at home with my parents, laid up in bed, too sick to even attend school anymore. His immune system was shot, and I'd been forced to make the decision to pull Hannah from the daycare she loved to keep her from bringing germs home to her brother. She would have loved that damn Spring Fling too.

Strings of uncaught cotton candy floated in the air while the sporadic grinding of the snow cone machine interrupted the sound of Disney classics playing on a loudspeaker. A circle of little girls was *letting it go* when movement to my right caught my attention.

A woman ducked under the ropes partitioning the grilling area off, and her long, black hair whipped into her face as the wind curled around her.

"Hi," she said, her voice almost robotic.

As she fought to get the hair out of her face, I took the moment to rake my gaze over her thin frame. She was cute, understated, in a pair of dark jeans and an oversized hoodie that hugged her about as well as a lawn and leaf bag, and not even a hint of makeup covered her olive complexion. She reminded me of a girl I might see cozied up in one of the overstuffed chairs at a coffee shop in the middle of August, desperately pretending it was December: sweatshirt wrapped around her, eyes aimed down at a book, plump lips sipping a steaming-hot chocolate while the hot sun blazed in from the window behind her.

Intriguing enough for you to notice.

Closed off enough to keep you from approaching.

Beautiful enough to keep you thinking about her for days after.

"Um…hi," she repeated awkwardly when I continued to silently stare at her. "Pickle jar?"

I blinked and traced my gaze down her delicate arm to her hand. Sure enough, she was offering me an empty pickle jar, complete with a green top, a narrow slit carved out of the center.

"It's a ticket-holder thingy. Rita told me you'd need one."

I raked my gaze over her again, noticing a small line of sweat beading on her forehead. And because I obviously needed to max myself out on awkwardness for the day, I told her, "You're hot."

*Jesus, Porter.*

Her eyebrows shot up, and she set the jar down on the side of the grill. "Right. Well, I'll let you get back to it."

"Shit. Wait. I'm sorry. That didn't come out right. What I meant to say is you have to *be* hot. It's, like, eighty degrees today."

"Right," she said dryly as she continued her retreat.

"Seriously, I didn't mean… Oh shit!" I yelled when flames shot up out of the grill.

Grabbing a bottle of water, I dumped it onto the flames. Then I threw my hand up in front of my face when it caused them to flare out to the sides.

Yep. It was official. I was going to set the park on fire.

Good news: There was medical personnel onsite.

Bad news: I could kiss that appointment for Travis goodbye.

"Watch out." The woman appeared at my side, sliding into the narrow space in front of me. Her long, dark hair smacked me in the face as she twisted the knobs until the fire died down.

A ragged breath of relief flew from my lungs. "Christ, that could have been bad."

She turned to face me, sporting a scowl that I had no doubt could cause frostbite.

With a tight smile, I said, "I think the grill is defective."

"The grill or you?" she retorted.

"*Definitely* the grill."

Swiftly, she lifted the box of burnts off the ground and pointedly thrust it in my direction. "You do know that the cow is already dead, right? There's no need to punish it any further." The words kinda-sorta sounded like they might have been a joke, but her voice held no humor.

I narrowed my eyes, trying to figure out how to respond. My gut told me to be a dick, but my better judgment won out.

"You're rude," I stated.

She twisted her lips. "Says the man staring at me like he just got out of prison."

I wanted to laugh. I liked dry humor, and she wasn't wrong. I was absolutely checking her out.

But again…I had no fucking idea if she was even trying to be funny.

The woman was unreadable.

Until she wasn't.

The song on the loudspeaker changed and a round of children's squeals and cheers signaled their exuberant approval.

It happened so fast that, had I been anyone else, I would have missed it.

But it was there. And I recognized it immediately.

I saw it in the mirror every morning when I woke up and every night before I went to bed.

Lowering my voice, I inched toward her, desperately hoping for a better look. "Are you okay?"

"Of course," she clipped.

Cool, calm, collected.

*Hiding in plain sight.*

It was almost as intriguing as it was heartbreaking.

She peeked up as I hovered over her. "What are you doing?" she snapped, swaying away from me.

"Nothing," I replied.

*Everything*, I thought.

I loomed closer and her dark gaze lifted to mine.

*Holy. Shit.*

There it was, blazing in her eyes.

The emptiness.

*My* emptiness.

I'd perfected the ability to lock my every emotion away. Hiding them from not only the world, but myself as well. If

I didn't enable the pain and fear, they had no power over me. But, as the years had passed, the hollowness left behind had been worse.

My smile had become a mask for the kids.

My laugh a guise to throw my family off the beaten path.

Going through the motions of carrying on—all the while, I was withering away.

And there it was, like a beacon of light shining within her too.

"Hi," I whispered as if we were long-lost friends.

She blinked and craned her head back to peer up at me. "Hi?"

She thought I was insane, and I couldn't give the first damn. Hell, I thought I was insane too.

But that didn't stop me from smiling and repeating, "Hi." When she stared up at me blankly, I added, "For the record, I do have other words in my vocabulary, but I seem to be stuck on that one right now."

The tiniest smile I'd ever seen played at her lips.

She'd been beautiful before. But, in that second, she became extraordinary.

Her deep-brown eyes flashed back and forth between mine, searching. "You're freaking me out."

I chuckled. "You're kinda freaking me out too."

"Maybe you could…back up, then?"

Unmoving, I confirmed, "I absolutely could."

"Today?" she pressed, but she was still wearing that virtually undetectable smile.

No. This woman wasn't rude. Or bitchy. She was simply surviving.

Just like me.

Shaking my head, I forced myself to snap out of it before I scared her off. "Yeah. Sorry about that."

She nervously looked away only for her gaze to bounce back to mine. "For what part? Ruining the burgers or challenging the laws of personal space?"

I blew out a hard breath and went for humor. "Ruining the burgers?" I pointed to the box of rejects. "You might call that burnt, but I call it food safety. No one is getting E. coli on my watch."

She aimed that smile up at me. And it wasn't fake. It wasn't a mask. It wasn't even hollow.

It was downright playful.

And unbelievably stunning.

I kept talking for fear it would disappear. "Really, it's a genetic condition. I didn't get the gene for charbroiling raw meat."

"Did you get the gene for *passing* raw meat?" she asked, the side of her mouth twitching as she tried to wipe away my fucking favorite smile.

I grinned. "I got two of those, actually." I twisted my hands in the air and made a show of walking backwards to the cooler. After retrieving a stainless-steel tray, I carried it back to her.

"Wow," she breathed. "I don't think I've ever seen anyone carry meat like that before."

I shrugged. "I harness my powers for good."

"The world needs more heroes like you," she told the grill as that tiny smile spread impossibly wide.

The hairs on the back of my neck stood on end as if I'd witnessed a miracle.

"I do what I can for humanity."

And then she gave me one better.

A real, honest-to-God giggle rang through the air.

Fuck. This woman.

She started placing patties in a rectangle around the outside edges of the heat. "So, tell me, Grill Master Max. How'd you get this job?"

"Surprisingly enough, a dead dog."

Her head snapped up. "Please, God, tell me that's not your secret ingredient."

I barked a laugh. "Hardly. That right there is a mixture of Wagyu, USDA Prime, and Argentinean free-range sirloin."

She curled her lip. "Wagyu?"

I winked arrogantly. "It's a thing. Look it up."

She pointed at me with the tongs. "Oh, I will, and if I find out it's a breed of canine, I'm calling the health department."

Chuckling, I opened my mouth to give what was surely going to be a witty response, but everything suddenly changed.

"Lucas," a woman called.

My gorgeous woman spun so fast that you would have thought she was on fire.

Concerned, I followed her gaze to a little boy. He was no older than two, toddling over, his mother hot on his heels.

"Slow down, buddy," the mother cooed, scooping the child up before he had a chance to get under the rope.

The whole interaction was utterly innocent, which only made it that much more puzzling when the spatula fell from her hand and she stumbled back a step.

On pure instinct, I caught her bicep to keep her from hitting the grill. "Hey, are you okay?"

"Yeah," she lied with a practiced ease, her gaze never leaving the departing mother.

Her chest heaved, and her anxiety was palpable, sparking mine to life as well.

As she swayed into me, her shoulder tucked under my arm and her hand clung to my forearm.

Sliding my arm around her hips, I pulled her closer and took some of her weight.

"Are you…" I trailed off. There was no point finishing the question. She wasn't okay in any fashion.

I knew that feeling too.

"Lucas," she whispered on a jagged breath, her hand coming up to cover her mouth as though she were trying to catch the word before it had fully escaped.

I glanced to where the woman and her child had disappeared into the crowd and asked, "Do you know that little boy?"

It took her several seconds to reply. "No. I don't," she whispered like it was a pained confession.

And then I lost her all over again.

As if someone had snapped their fingers to break her trance, she suddenly pushed out of my arms. "I'm good."

I frowned when the shake of her hands said otherwise. "Listen—"

"Really. I'm fine." Tilting her head back, she met my gaze and it was one of the most incredible things I'd ever witnessed. And not in a good way.

A wall came down, dividing her from me—and the rest of the world. Her eyes grew distant, and while her shoulders fell only a fraction of an inch, that slight change was enough to transform her from the beautiful woman with the secret smile to a shattered woman barely able to stand.

It was familiar.

Too familiar.

"I have to go," she whispered.

"Don't." I reached out for her, my pulse quickening.

She dodged my touch. "Can you…uh…do me a favor and tell Rita that I got called up to the hospital?"

"Stay and help me cook. I'll drive you there after we finish," I bargained, worry thick in my voice. She didn't need to be driving anywhere. Not like that.

She shook her head and started away, my anxiety growing with her every step.

"Wait," I called. But what the hell else was I going to say?

Maybe I had it all wrong.

Maybe we didn't share a mutual pain.

Maybe I was doing what I did best and allowing my worst-case-scenario mind to run the show.

Or maybe I had it exactly right and was allowing her to slip through my fingers when she needed someone the most.

"Shit," I mumbled as she jogged away, not even leaving so much as her name behind.

"Sorry I'm late," Tanner said, ducking under the rope.

A combination of shock and relief washed over me. "What are you doing here?"

He chuckled and lifted the lid on the grill, shaking his head as his gaze drifted down to my cardboard box. "Jesus. I was just fucking with you about not coming. I didn't seriously think you'd start cooking."

I wanted to be pissed that my brother was such a jackass,

but my mind was still with the despondent woman I'd let escape.

Suddenly, Rita's voice joined the conversation. "Hey. How'd it go?"

I swallowed hard and tried to get my head back in the game. I was there for Travis. I couldn't afford to forget that.

"Well, I almost lit the place on fire." I hooked my thumb over my shoulder at Tanner. "But we should be good now."

"No. I meant with Charlotte."

I blinked, her words slowly filtering through me—before crushing me to the ground. "Charlotte?" I asked, because there was no way I'd heard her correctly.

Her eyes gentled, and her lips thinned. "She told you no, didn't she?"

*No fucking way.*

I closed my eyes and dropped my chin to my chest. "Please, God, tell me that wasn't Dr. Mills?"

"Shit," she mumbled. "I sent her over so you could talk to her. I figured you already had when I saw her take off."

"No," I laughed without humor. "I didn't know who she was!"

Reading my emotions, Tanner moved in beside me. "Well, send her back over. I'd love to meet her."

"She left. She had to go to the hospital," I announced, planting one hand on my hip and raking the other through my hair.

*Son of a bitch!*

How could I have let this happen?

"Porter, honey," Rita soothed. "If it's any consolation, she was never going to agree to see your boy."

After sinking down onto the cooler, I dropped my elbows to my knees. "You don't know that. I could have persuaded her."

"We'll figure it out," Tanner said confidently, patting me on the thigh. "Whatever you need, I'll make it happen."

So maybe my brother wasn't a total jackass, but his promise didn't exactly fill me with hope, either.

"I'm really sorry," Rita said. "It's just Charlotte. She's..."

Broken.

Ruined.

Shattered.

Just. Fucking. Like. Me.

But my son needed her.

Visions of Travis sitting on the side of the tub, drenched in sweat, heaving for a single breath, assaulted me. He'd been released from the hospital after one night *this time.*

But what about the next time?

And the next?

What about the one fucking time he didn't come home?

Panic blasted through me.

Okay. I could figure this out. What choice did I have?

"What hospital?" I asked, pushing to my feet.

"Uh..." Rita drawled, her wide eyes flashing between me and my brother. "I'm not sure I can divulge that information."

I took a step toward her, Tanner on my heels. "I'm not going to cause her any trouble. But, to be honest, she didn't look good when she rushed out of here. Something spooked her. Some kid named Lucas."

Rita gasped, and her face drained of color.

Her reaction fueled my fire.

"I just want to make sure she got to the hospital safely." And then do whatever the fuck I had to do to get my son into her office first thing on Monday morning. "I'll take her lunch."

Tanner took the cue and headed to his station, placing two fresh burgers on the grill.

Folding my hands in prayer, I lifted them to Rita. "Please."

Her face grew soft. "It's not going to work."

"Maybe not. But, worst case, she gets something to eat and I get a door shut in my face. Let me try. That's all I'm asking."

Consideration danced through her features for a second longer. "Oh, all right. Emory…and medium rare, extra mustard and pickles."

Hope exploded within me as I swung my head to my brother, a victorious grin pulling at both of our mouths.

"Five minutes to plate!" he called out.

Yeah, okay. He wasn't an asshole at all.

# EIGHT

## Charlotte

"SAYONARA!" HEATHER CALLED OUT AS A NURSE'S assistant wheeled Mr. Clark to the elevator. A round of laughter sounded behind her.

"Keep it professional," I scolded under my breath as I continued to read through the on-call's notes from the night before.

He knew me well and had left a novel's worth of information to explain his every decision with my patient. Which honestly could have been summed up with: I followed your orders from the night before. Whatever. I liked the extra information. I stared at the words on the page, reading them and then rereading them, unable to focus.

That guy from the fling was hijacking my thoughts.

A chill traveled down my spine. *"Hi,"* he'd said.

One word. One syllable. Two letters.

In my thirty-three years of life, I'd probably heard that

word a million times.

But not like that. Never like that. It had echoed in my head as I'd driven to the hospital.

It was stupid. He was stupid. I was stupid for reading into it. So what—a guy was awkwardly flirting with me? It happened.

But this guy…

Yes. I'd bolted like the emotionally unstable crazy woman I so obviously was. That was nothing new. But, for reasons I'd never be able to explain, he had come with me.

At least, in my memories.

I closed my eyes and sucked in a deep breath.

His crooked grin.

His blue eyes, which had bored so deeply into me that I'd momentarily gotten lost.

His ridiculous jokes.

The smiles I couldn't contain.

His messy hair and his chiseled jaw.

His large hand on my hip.

His strong arm supporting me as I'd fought to stay in the present.

His low, gravelly voice.

"Hi."

I smiled to myself.

"Can I help you?" Heather asked, sliding her rolling chair over beside mine.

"Actually, I'm here to see Dr. Mills."

My head snapped up and I found a pair of topaz blue eyes framed with thick lashes staring down at me.

*Oh shit.*

"Grill Master Max," I greeted, fighting the absurd instinct to smooth my hair down. "What are you doing here?"

He was still tall, not like that had changed in the half hour since I'd seen him last. But his disheveled, blond hair, longer on the top than on the sides, had been combed and he'd shed his filthy apron, revealing a clean and crisp, white Polo that stretched around his biceps. I mean, not that I was looking or anything. His arms were just there...attached to his shoulders.

Wide and muscular shoulders.

*Shit.*

"Well, after you ran out on me, the grill exploded. I was down in the emergency room—"

I shot to my feet, sending my rolling chair sailing across the room. "What!"

He chuckled. "I'm kidding. I brought you lunch." He set a heaving plastic bag on the counter, the smell of dear-God-deliciousness wafting out of it.

My stomach rumbled in approval, but my mind was slightly more cautious. "Why?"

He narrowed his eyes, but his grin never faltered. "Why not?"

*Because you don't know me.*

*Because I damn near had a nervous breakdown at the sound of my son's name earlier when, for a split second, I looked at that little boy and hoped he could be mine, despite the fact that he was at least eight years too young.*

*Because my life is so fucking complicated that you would suffocate in my reality.*

I kept all of that to myself. "Aren't you supposed to be serving up charred leather and tire rubber to dozens of unsuspecting victims right about now?"

His eyes twinkled with mischief. "If that were not incredibly accurate, I'd be offended. But no. My brother is the chef in the family, and he finally showed up to take over. Including cooking this." He pushed the bag a fraction of an inch closer. "I assure you there is no tire rubber involved." He didn't say anything else as he stared at me, his assessing eyes scanning my face as though he were trying to read my answer before I'd even formulated it.

"No tire rubber involved? That's quite the sales pitch," I smarted.

"I know. I'm having posters made up and everything."

I cut my gaze to the floor so he wouldn't see my smile.

"So what do you say? Me. You. A table in the cafeteria. Grilled-to-perfection Wagyu?"

I bit the inside of my cheek. "Sorry. I don't eat dog."

He laughed. "That's a good standard to live by. But Wagyu is Japanese beef. It's highly desired because it's genetically predisposed to intense marbling, thus producing a high percentage of oleaginous unsaturated fat."

My mouth fell open. "You know all of that about Japanese beef but you don't know how to grill a burger?"

He lifted a shoulder in a half shrug. "What can I say? My parents failed me. The internet did not."

I laughed—and not a quiet giggle. It was a real-life belly laugh. While I didn't snort, I'm not sure it could have been any less attractive if I had.

He didn't seem to mind though. His lips stretched, revealing at least four years of orthodontics and negative amounts of coffee and red wine.

"Well…thanks. You really didn't have to bring it all the way down here." I reached for the bag, but he pulled it out of my reach.

"I did if I wanted to have lunch with you."

Nerves bloomed in my stomach and the word "No" rolled off my tongue on pure instinct.

"No?" he repeated in surprise.

Funny, the same question echoed in my head.

It wasn't that I didn't *want* to have lunch with him. It was just that I wasn't prepared. You couldn't spring lunch on a girl. I was still reeling from my near nervous breakdown. Yes. I was starving. But he'd probably want to have a conversation. Oh dear God. What if he actually expected me to chime in with opinions and small talk of my own?

Nope. Not happening.

"I'm kinda busy right now," I lied.

His smile deflated. "Oh. Okay."

Guilt rolled through me. Damn it. I should have offered him a gift card.

"I'm sorry. You know how it is. Work. Work. Work."

He waved my apology off. "Yeah. My job's the same way. You. Saving lives. Me… Ordering cocktail napkins?" He twisted his lips adorably. "No. You know what? It's not even similar."

I tipped my head to the side. "You order cocktail napkins for a living?"

"That's what it feels like sometimes, but no, I own a restaurant. Well, actually, two restaurants."

My eyes must have flashed with surprise, because he lifted his hands and placated, "But I assure you I don't cook at either of them."

A laugh bubbled from my throat.

What the hell was I doing? I'd vowed to myself that it was time for a change.

I'd even promised that I would *be* the change. And there I was, turning a man down, who for all intents and purposes seemed like a good guy, because it was easier to stay in the darkness than it was to brave the sunlight. So much of my energy was spent trying to exist in a world that never slowed down. Maybe I just needed to speed up.

Those damn baby steps were only causing me to fall further and further behind.

This guy—this lunch—could be my first giant step.

What could it possibly hurt? Right?

Famous last words, huh?

But, then again, for ten years, my life had been ruled by *words*.

Fear. Guilt. Terror. Anxiety. Solitude. Longing.

It was time to let some feelings in.

After flipping Mr. Clark's file closed with one hand, I slid it onto the top discharge pile. "You know what? I can take a break."

His whole handsome face lit. "Really?"

"Really," I confirmed.

"Thank God," he breathed in a strange mixture of relief and excitement. "I should probably introduce myself, huh?" He thrust a hand over the desk dividing us. "Hi. I'm Porter Reese."

I didn't know it yet. But those four simple *words* changed my life all over again.

# NINE

## Porter

"So let me get this straight. Your brother is supposedly a famous chef named Tanner and the two of you named your restaurant The Porterhouse?" she asked then slipped a spoonful of potato salad into her mouth.

I laughed. "You can't argue with the winner of the Ninja Warrior course."

She blinked. But her lips tipped up in a breathtaking smile.

After I'd completed the grueling—and slightly terrifying—task of convincing her to have lunch with me, Charlotte had led me through the hospital maze to the packed cafeteria. No one spoke their hellos as we walked past, but more than once, I caught hospital personnel doing an openmouthed double take. Though, if Charlotte noticed, she didn't let on. She kept her head down, eyes forward, and ignored the world.

I had to admit I was envious. I'd been trying for years to

accomplish that feat.

First stop on my way home was going to be to buy myself a flame-retardant suit because there were no ifs, ands, or buts about it—I was going to hell.

I'd yet to mention Travis or the appointment I so desperately needed from her, but that could come later. And there was absolutely going to be a later.

Charlotte Mills was fascinating.

She didn't talk much, but she wasn't quiet, either. She was very much present in the conversation, one sentence or sarcastic comment at a time. Engaging, but still withdrawn. The emptiness rolled like waves through her dark eyes, occasionally fading out of view as a subtle light flickered in the background.

I didn't know much about her other than the fact that she picked all the sesame seeds off her burger and used thick layers of mustard like most people would use ketchup.

But I was drawn to her in inexplicable ways.

She spoke my language, even if I didn't know why.

I'd gone there for Travis, first and foremost. But, somewhere around the point when she breathed my name, I knew I was going to have to multitask.

There wasn't a chance in hell I was walking out of that hospital without an appointment for myself too. Mine was going to be after hours and sans the hospital johnny.

Christ, she was cute.

Her smiles were reserved, but when she aimed them at me, it felt as though I'd conquered Mount Everest. I knew firsthand how arduous it was to produce a smile.

Not the one I displayed like an avatar.

A real one.

Gone was her hoodie, and in its place was an equally flattering scrub top. But I didn't care what she was wearing. Her being beautiful was nothing more than an incredibly nice by-product.

I wasn't a rash person by any stretch of the imagination, but I felt it with her—the common denominator I'd never found with anyone else.

Don't get me wrong. Love at first sight didn't exist. Soul mates were the likes of fairytales. And lust wasn't love, no matter how hard you tried to convince yourself otherwise.

Feelings faded. Obsessions got rerouted. True colors never stayed hidden for long.

So, while I was absolutely intrigued by this woman, I wasn't delusional enough to think it would ever be anything more than that. I was a numbers guy. She was only one woman out of the 3.7 billion on the planet. Statistically, I had a better chance of falling in love with a sheep than this broken woman. But I was also a believer that people entered your life for a reason and it was up to you to figure out why.

Yeah. I was going to hell, because before I gave her the chance to shoot me down about Travis, I was going to figure out why she'd entered mine.

"So, what are you naming the new restaurant?" she asked, pinching a bite off her burger before popping it into her mouth. She'd eaten nearly her entire sandwich in the same manner.

Seriously. Fucking cute.

I chuckled and leaned back against the padded cafeteria booth, my burger long since gone. "The Tannerhouse."

She lifted her hand to cover her mouth and mumbled

around her food. "Seriously?"

"Unfortunately, yes. And it gets worse. It's all one word. Tannerhouse. Like Porterhouse, only not actually a word."

She laughed, and the sound danced over my skin.

Fuck Mount Everest. That felt like I'd built a ladder straight to the heavens. (And yes, I'd realized exactly how goddamn cheesy that thought was. But fuck, it felt *that fucking good* when the sound of her laughter drew a laugh from my own throat.)

I tried not to stare at her mouth, but it was a futile effort. Her pink lips were a perfect crescent, pouty and pink.

While Charlotte didn't have the warmest demeanor, there was no mistaking the fact that everything about her was entirely feminine. Even the simple things, like the way she used two fingers to tuck her hair behind her ear or the way she set her fork down after every bite, were almost graceful.

When she caught me staring, her cheeks pinked and she looked down, her long, straight hair falling forward to curtain her face off.

My hands ached to brush it over her shoulder so I could see her again. Just as I was about to give in to the urge, she looked up, a new confidence blazing in her eyes.

"Your brother sounds like a character."

I nodded. "If, by character, you mean his life goal is to screw with me, then yes. He is a *huge* character."

"Is he older or younger?" she asked before pinching another tiny bite off her burger.

"Younger by two years."

"So that makes him, what, like, twenty-five, twenty-six?"

I wasn't the only one at that table flirting. Mine was

slightly more overt, but she wasn't fooling anyone.

Leaning forward on my elbows, I shot her a teasing side-eye. "Are you asking because you want to know how old *he* is or how old *I* am?"

Her face remained stoic. "Well, you said he was famous. So, clearly, I was asking about him."

She was kidding. Dry as the Sahara Desert. But I fucking loved it, so I remained stoic as well.

After picking my cell phone up, I opened the web browser. "He's thirty-two. You want to see a picture?"

"Absolutely." She leaned forward with mock interest.

I knew that it was mock because her heated gaze roamed over my arms and my shoulders when she thought I wasn't looking.

Shaking my head, I went to work searching through Google images for exactly the right picture. Passing it her way, I lied, "If you're interested, I could see if he's free for dinner tonight."

I would quite possibly light Tanner on fire before I'd let him anywhere near her.

"That sounds amazing. I'll rush home and..." She didn't finish the thought when her gaze landed on the screen. "Dear God," she whispered, covering her mouth with her hand. "He's an Adonis."

The picture was of Sloth from *The Goonies*.

"People say we look alike, but I don't see it."

"Oh, you don't look anything alike."

"No?" I smirked.

"Oh, no way. He's so much better looking than you are."

The smile that split my lips was unrivaled. But the real

surprise was when it traveled from my mouth through my body, igniting me in the most unfamiliar way.

"Obviously," I replied, reaching for my phone. "If you give me your number, I'll be happy to forward you the picture. You know, so you can stare at it later."

"Really?" she breathed. "Your kindness knows no bounds."

Swear to God, there wasn't an ounce of humor in her voice. I was so fucking impressed.

She pulled her phone out of her pocket and rattled a string of numbers off. I couldn't program those digits in quickly enough.

Flashing her a grin, I got busy typing a text out.

**Me**: Hey, it's Porter. AKA: Grill Master Max.

I looked up as her phone vibrated. "You should probably reply to that. It might be an insanely gorgeous man trying to ask you out."

Her lips twitched as she brought her phone up, her thumbs fluidly gliding over the screen.

**Her**: The ugly Reese brother?
**Me**: I prefer genetically challenged, but yes.

When I pressed send, I turned my attention back to her. And I had the absolute pleasure of witnessing that lip twitch transform into a full-blown grin.

**Her**: My sincerest apologies for my insensitivity.

Her head lifted to mine, and I dodged the eye contact by focusing on my phone.

**Me**: Accepted. Listen, so I was thinking…

I sent the picture of Sloth.

**Me**: I may not be an Adonis, but maybe you could do your good deed for the year and go on a pity date with me tonight?

She laughed softly as she typed.

**Her**: Sorry. I already did my good deed by having a pity lunch with a man today. He fed me dog.

I barked a laugh but kept my head down.

**Me**: Wow. He sounds terrible. I can't imagine eating my Wagyu terrier.

**Her**: Yeah. He was charming in an awkward way, but I have no doubt he's a serial killer. He tried to light me on fire the first time we met.

My head snapped up. "Oh come on! I wasn't trying to set you on fire!" I exclaimed, placing my phone on the table.

She let out a loud laugh and followed suit, shoving her phone back into her pocket.

We sat in silence for several seconds. She poked at her potato salad with a spoon, while I stared at her, wishing she would give me her gaze back. Finally, I got up the nerve to slide my palm across the table until it covered her hand.

"You think I'm charming, huh?"

"I also think you're a serial killer," she told the potato salad.

Rubbing my thumb over the back of her hand, I asked, "So, just to be clear, where do we stand on the whole dinner thing?"

She looked up and her playful gaze had dimmed. "Porter, listen." She started to pull her hand away, but I refused to let go. "I'm not sure what Rita told you about me, but—"

"Rita didn't tell me anything."

"Right," she said dismissively. "You just happen to know where I was and how I eat my burger?"

*And that you refuse to treat children.*

"Okay, so Rita told me a little. But that's not why I want to have dinner with you."

She leaned back, slipping her hand from under mine, and crossed her arms over her chest. "I think you're a really sweet guy, but you should know I'm completely emotionally unavailable."

"No, you're not," I replied nonchalantly, reaching for her hand again.

She dodged my touch. "Oh, I'm not?"

"You aren't emotionally unavailable. You're emotionally closed off. Those are two totally different things."

She scoffed. "You don't know me."

After quickly sliding out of the booth, I swung around until I was sitting next to her.

"Wh…what are you doing?" she stammered, scooting over.

I followed her until her back hit the wall. Her leg was crooked up on the bench between us, so I slid my arm across the back of her seat and leaned forward until our upper bodies were mere inches apart. Her breathing sped, and my heart raced.

"I know you better than you think."

She opened her mouth to argue, but I didn't let her get a word in edgewise.

"You smile for people because it makes them comfortable, but it makes you feel like a fraud. You go through the motions of living but only so people will stop asking if you're doing okay. You laugh to remind yourself that you can still physically make the sound, even though you're so fucking numb you don't feel it. And you keep to yourself not because you like to be alone, but rather because you're the only person who truly understands."

Her mouth fell open and a soft gasp hitched her breath. "How…how do you know that?"

I finally gave in to the urge and tucked a strand of her soft, silky hair behind her ear. Then I cupped her cheek. "Because they're the same goddamn things I do every day."

She swallowed hard and then cut her eyes off to the side. "And let me guess. You want to sit around and commiserate with me because you think we both have issues? I guarantee you we're not as similar as you think."

"I know. And I assure you I have zero interest in commiserating with you. I wouldn't understand your demons any more than you would understand my personal circle of hell."

Her sad eyes flicked back to mine. "Then what do you want?"

I sucked in a deep breath that did nothing to calm the eternal storm brewing within me. "Just a little company in the darkness. No questions. No judgments. No faking it."

Her mouth fell open, and anxiety painted her face.

It was risky, coming on to her like that. Of all the fucked-up people I'd met over the last few years, only about a quarter of them knew they were fucked up.

My chest tightened as I waited for her reaction. There was no middle ground when you cornered a woman like that. She was going to either explode into an angry fury or melt into my arms. I prayed for the latter, but the former wouldn't stop me. Determination was like that. And, when it came to Charlotte Mills, determination was my middle name.

Nervously, I licked my lips, and much to my elation, her gaze dropped at the action.

Victory was within my reach.

She couldn't heal me. And I couldn't heal her.

But sometimes, when the overwhelming weight of gravity had you pinned to the Earth, two hours of simple conversation with no pressure to pretend was the only reprieve people like us were ever going to get.

Gliding my thumb over her bottom lip, I ordered on a low rumble, "Dinner, Charlotte. Say yes."

# TEN

## Charlotte

WITH SHAKY HANDS, I SMOOTHED MY BLACK BLOUSE down. No freaking clue what the material was or the shape to describe it. But it was sleeveless, not a scrub top, and it made me look like I had boobs. The trifecta of amazing when it came to my wardrobe.

On a breathy sigh, I'd agreed to dinner with Porter.

*No questions.*

*No judgments.*

*No faking it.*

The word *no* hadn't been in my vocabulary after an offer like that. It'd felt like I'd been waiting my entire life for someone to give me that out.

*Just a little company in the darkness.*

My heart hadn't stopped pounding since he'd slid into my side of the booth. His large body pressed against mine as those daunting, blue eyes had held me captive. My lids fluttered closed as I remembered the heat from his palm on my face, his fingerprints branding me.

After I'd left the hospital, I'd promptly gone to the mall and burned a hole in my debit card. Twelve tops I hadn't bothered trying on—all of which were black, only one of which (the one I was wearing) fit—and two pairs of black pants—both of which fit, only one of which made my ass look good (hence why I was wearing those)—later, I'd gone home. The nerves were nearly paralyzing when I pulled into my driveway. I had two hours before I was supposed to meet Porter. If I stuck to my normal getting-ready routine, that meant I had one hour—and forty-five minutes to talk myself out of going. Throwing the car in reverse, I headed back to the mall to see if the hair place could squeeze me in for a blowout.

They did. It looked incredible. Which meant my simple-splash-of-makeup face looked like shit. So I swung by the MAC counter on the way out.

By the time I walked through the heavy wooden doors at The Porterhouse, I looked like a new woman. Unfortunately, it wasn't as easy to dress the inside of me up to match. I wanted to be there. To see Porter again. But old habits were hard to break. I'd mentally stockpiled at least a dozen excuses for why I had to leave before our salads. (Okay, fine! Two of them would enable me to make a break for it before we'd even ordered drinks.)

The moment I heard his deep, gravelly voice, I knew I'd wasted my time.

"Charlotte," he greeted behind me as I stood at the busy hostess stand, waiting for my turn.

Whirling around, I found him prowling toward me, a

smile on his face, unmistakable heat in his eyes.

My stomach dipped as I raked my gaze down his body. Porter was tall, probably around six-three, and while he didn't carry a suit of muscle, his every curve was toned and hard. His built shoulders strained against the confinement of his white button-down. And, with his sleeves rolled up, stopping below his elbow, his powerfully veined forearms were on full display. He'd been attractive at the hospital. But, God, he was in an entirely different category now.

"Jesus," he breathed, stopping in front of me. "You…are stunning."

His hands landed on my hips as he dipped to kiss my cheek.

"Hi," I whispered, peeking up at him.

He grinned. "Hi."

We silently stared at each other for several seconds as the waiting crowd carried on around us. I was more content in that quiet moment than I had been in years.

*No questions.*

*No judgments.*

*No faking it.*

"I'm glad you came," he said, releasing my hips, and backing away a step.

The absence was staggering.

I swallowed hard. "I'm excited to see where you order cocktail napkins."

He chuckled. "Smartass."

After grabbing a menu from behind the hostess stand, he placed a hand on my lower back and led me through the restaurant. I had to give it to him; The Porterhouse was a sight to be seen. Tall booths lined the walls, while rustic, distressed tables created an aisle down the center. At the back, it T'd off to the left and the right, revealing smaller, slightly more secluded rooms. Brass lanterns with flickering candles adorned the tables, while the bright, white plates and shiny silverware gave it a classic Southern elegance.

Clearly, I wasn't the only one who thought the place was amazing. Every table was full and dozens of waiters and waitresses bustled around us.

With a sweeping hand, Porter motioned toward an open booth.

"This place is incredible," I said, sliding in on one side.

"Thanks. I'll let Tanner know you think so." He shrugged sheepishly and placed the menu in front of me. "I lost the Ninja Warrior course the day we competed for the ambiance. If it had been up to me, we'd have paper tablecloths and crayons."

I laughed softly and set my purse beside me.

Tilting my head up, I saw him staring at me, a one-sided grin lighting his face.

My cheeks flamed red all over again.

And then he sat down…

Like, on the same side of the booth…

As in right *next* to me.

Who did that?

Oh God. Maybe I would need one of those excuses after all.

And then it got worse.

He angled to the side and leaned across me.

"Uhh…" I drawled.

Pressing against the back of the seat, I tried to get out of his way, but his large upper body was wedged between me and the table, his hand doing God only knew what underneath.

During all of this, I would be remiss if I didn't admit to secretly sniffing him. (Come on. He was the one sitting on my side of the booth, which everyone including a socially inept person such as myself knew was a major dating faux pas. And then if you add in the weird leaning-into-my-lap thing... smelling him was the least of our problems.)

But, dear God, did he smell good.

While I mentally congratulated myself on suppressing a moan, Porter suddenly sat up, his cell phone dangling from the end of a charger.

"Sorry. My phone died earlier while I was waiting on you." He climbed out of the booth and moved to the bench across from me.

*Praise. God.*

"Were you waiting long?" I asked nervously. And, judging by the gorgeous smirk that tipped his lips, my cheeks had flashed from pink to red.

"Nope. You were right on time." His eyes were bright as he confidently folded his hands in front of him and stared at me in the most unnerving way possible.

And this was Porter. It seemed that unnerving me was his favorite pastime.

Lifting the menu, I pretended to search the pages. "I usually am."

"Good to know," he mumbled, but I could still feel his gaze burning into me.

A chill traveled down my spine with as much excitement

as discomfort.

Why was he staring at me like that?

Just as I decided to dig into my old jar of excuses and make a break for it, a young, attractive waitress appeared at the side of the table.

"Hey, Porter. You eating tonight?"

"Yeah," he replied. "Charlotte, you want a drink?"

"A glass of wine. White. House is fine." I must have said it a little too eagerly, because Porter chuckled.

"Bring us a bottle of Sav Blanc. Australian. And I'll take a Hendrix and tonic."

"Two limes?" she chirped.

Though it was a damn miracle I heard her at all, because right then, Porter reached across the table and hooked my fingers with his.

"That'd be great," he said.

I felt her presence leave. Not that I looked up to confirm or anything. That would have required me to make eye contact, and I feared that my cheeks would go up in flames. And, beyond that, I was too busy pretending to be enthralled with the menu rather than the fact that he was now *holding my hand*.

Christ. I should have known better than to go on a date.

"Charlotte," he called softly.

"What do you recommend?" I asked.

His thumb brushed over my knuckles. "Charlotte," he repeated.

"I haven't had a decent steak in a while." I turned the page, not seeing a single word.

"Charlotte," he repeated, this time louder.

Without any way to ignore him longer, I looked up. "Yeah?"

His handsome face was warm with understanding. "Relax."

I allowed the menu to fall to the table and grinned sheepishly. "I'm sorry. I haven't been on a date in a really long time. At least, not a good one. Rita set me up with her hairdresser's son a few months back. But he was an accountant, so I snuck out the bathroom window."

His eyebrows popped up, but I carried on because, well, he was still staring at me and *still* stroking his thumb over the back of my hand in a way that felt divine—and slightly petrifying.

"I work twenty-four hours a day. And live and breathe my career. I don't know what Rita told you about me, but I can assure you it wasn't true. I'm not funny or interesting like she loves to tell men. In truth, my life is a mess. I'm a boring homebody who reads medical journals for entertainment and survives on microwave dinners for one. I appreciate you asking me out to dinner. I really do. But I'm not sure I can do this."

He continued to stare at me, but his eyes took on a humorous glint.

Great. He was laughing at me.

I needed to get the hell out of there. But first I had to get my hand back.

Grabbing my purse, I gave my hand a tug, but he kept it pinned to the table.

"He was an accountant?"

Of all the questions I figured he'd ask after my little trip to the restaurant confessional, that was not one I'd considered.

"Yeah. It was terrible."

He laughed. "And you thought you were boring."

I snapped my gaze back to his, a smile pulling at my lips. "Right? I almost fell asleep on him."

He finally released my hand and took the menu from in front of me, moving it out of the way. "I'll do what I can to keep you awake tonight. I retired from accounting a few years back." He winked.

*Shit!*

I bit my bottom lip.

He chuckled. "Relax. I didn't ask you to dinner for entertainment." He dug into his pocket and retrieved a pen before writing something on a cocktail napkin. "I don't need a song and dance. I said no faking it and I meant it. If you want to sit there and stare at the menu until you memorize it, I'm more than happy to sit here and watch you do it." He flashed me a smile but kept his eyes aimed at whatever he was writing. Or maybe he was drawing? I couldn't tell. "You want to talk, I'll talk. You want to sit in silence, fine by me." He finally slid the cocktail napkin toward me.

It was some kind of map. Arrows started at a small star at the top, continuing through the maze of lines before separating out into two different paths.

I was still trying to make heads or tails of his sketch when he folded his hand over the top of mine. A-GAIN!

What the hell was up with this guy and holding hands? I'd known Porter for less than twenty-four hours and I'd already had more physical contact with him than I'd had with anyone else in years.

"Charlotte, I would love it if you'd stay through the *entire* dinner. Maybe even through dessert and coffee too. But, if you decide to leave, I should warn you that there isn't a window in the women's restroom." He remained serious as he pointed at one of the arrows. "Your best bet will be the emergency exit at the end of the hall." He traced his finger across the napkin to the end of the other path. "Or the one at the back of the building."

Covering my mouth with a hand, I tried to hide my smile, but it was a worthless attempt, especially when he grinned.

He continued. "Let me be the first to inform you. I'm boring too. And I haven't been on a date in years. All kidding aside, you might need that map in an hour. But you're beautiful. And smart. And, regardless of whether you think you are, you're funny too. So I'm going to sit here for however long you're willing to stay and hope like hell that cocktail napkin ends up in the trash."

Jesus. Where did this guy come from?

We sat in silence, his left hand on top of my right, my heart racing, his gaze never drifting from mine, his blues locked on my browns.

When the waitress returned, she talked.

Porter answered.

But I sat there, reveling in the warmth that I hadn't experienced since the chill of reality had devoured me.

"So, what do you say?" Porter asked as the waitress watched me expectantly.

"I'm sorry… What?"

"I asked if you were gonna stay long enough to eat?"

Damn it. I absolutely was. Porter might have wanted company in the darkness. But, with a single taste of the warmth, I wanted to bask in the sunlight.

"Depends. What kind of dessert do you have for after dinner?" I asked, turning my hand over to intertwine our fingers.

His eyes darkened as he purred, "Anything you want, Charlotte."

"Chocolate cake?"

"World famous."

Without a word, I crumpled his cocktail napkin map into a ball with my free hand.

He smiled. Mine was bigger.

"Okay, Megan," he said to the waitress. "The lady will have the German Shepherd T-bone."

A loud laugh sprang from my throat.

"What?" He feigned ignorance. "You seemed to like the Wagyu today. I figured we might as well stick with canine."

"Uh..." the waitress drawled in disgust.

I laughed again. Real. Honest. Laughter.

And I felt it all the way down to the core of my soul.

That was the exact moment I should have realized Porter Reese was dangerous.

But I was too lost in his sultry eyes and his heart-stopping smile to give it a second thought.

For two hours, Porter and I talked, using actual *words.* And not a single one of them destroyed me. They were light and fun but no less life changing. It had been too long since I'd allowed myself a night like that. I turned my cell phone off, drank wine, and had a fantastic meal with an incredible man.

Porter kept his end of the bargain. He didn't ask questions or cast any judgments.

And I kept mine by not faking a single smile. I didn't need

to. My cheeks were aching before I'd finished my salad.

For those two hours, the world kept spinning, only this time, I wasn't frozen in place or sprinting to keep up.

Porter and I spun together.

At the end of the night, after a giant piece of chocolate cake with two forks and two cups of coffee, he walked me to my car.

Not surprisingly, he held my hand the whole way.

Definitely surprisingly, he brushed his lips against mine in an all too brief kiss.

And then, as I climbed into my car and waved at him from the wrong side of the windshield, that warmth didn't just wash over me—it consumed me.

# ELEVEN

## Charlotte

**Porter**: Did you make it home safely?

**Me**: I did. I just got into bed actually.

**Porter:** Funny you should mention that…how do you feel about tacos?

**Me:** In bed?

**Porter:** What? No! We've been on two dates. Do I look easy to you?

**Me:** You just said "Funny you should mention that…how do you feel about tacos?" After I said I just got into bed.

**Porter:** Ohhhh…see I thought you said, "I just got a burrito actually."

**Me**: Uh…I typed it. I didn't say it.

**Porter**: Fine! I didn't have a good transition from bed to see if you wanted to go have tacos with me tomorrow.

I laughed and rolled to my side, kicking the covers off to

combat the new warmth coursing through my veins.

**Me:** I don't know. If you count the Spring Fling, that's like four dates in two days.

**Porter:** I know. You can't get enough of me. Don't worry. I find it endearing.

**Me**: Well, that's a relief.

**Porter**: Okay. Okay. You don't need to beg. Yes, I'll have tacos with you tomorrow at noon. I know a guy who knows a guy who knows a guy who can get us reservations at Taco Bell.

I smiled so wide I feared it would split my face.

**Me**: I knew dating a restaurateur would have its perks.

**Porter**: What can I say? I'm quite a catch. Now, say yes to lunch.

**Me**: Why are you always trying to force me into having meals with you?

**Porter:** Because if I left our dates up to you, we'd be eating tacos in bed. That's at least a sixth-date kind of activity. Slow down there, Mills.

My laugh echoed off the bare walls of my bedroom. Closing my eyes, I sucked in a breath and sank deep into my bed.

**Me**: You're right. My mind was clearly in the Mexican gutter. My deepest heartfelt apologies.

**Porter**: Forgiven. Listen, I just got a text from my guy who knows a guy who knows a guy and unfortunately Taco

Bell is fully booked for tomorrow. However, he was able to get us a table for two at Antojitos.

Antojitos wasn't your average restaurant—it was an experience. The whole place was decorated like a quaint road in Mexico, and waiters wandered around dressed as street vendors offering a plethora of authentic Mexican fare. Every day, the menu was different, but people raved about it. It was always delicious. They didn't take reservations, so there was usually a line wrapped around the block.

**Me**: That's not fair. You can't tease a girl with Taco Bell and then try to use Antojitos as a sad second choice.

**Porter**: I know. I know. And to make it up to you, I'd be willing to eat your tacos in bed on our FIFTH date.

**Porter**: Also…I JUST realized how filthy that sounded. I swear I didn't mean it like that.

I barked a laugh and paused my fingers over my keyboard when I saw the text bubble pop up. He was typing again.

**Porter**: I mean…unless you did. In which case, we can do tacos in bed any time you'd like.

**Porter**: Unless you were talking about real tacos, in which case the crumbs sound like a nightmare.

**Porter**: Actually, can you do me a favor and delete the last four messages from me without reading them? M'kay thanks.

Tears—*actual* tears—were in my eyes. I was laughing *that* hard.

**Porter**: Christ. Why aren't you responding now?

**Me**: Because it's more fun to watch you sweat.

**Porter**: Are you laughing?

**Me**: Yep.

**Porter**: That makes it almost worth the embarrassment.

Yeah. Okay. We were talking about eating tacos in bed (which was only slightly less horrifying than sitting on the same side of the booth), but I'll be damned if that warmth didn't fill me again.

**Me**: Antojitos sounds amazing. I have to swing by my office in the morning, so I'll meet you there at noon.

**Porter**: Sounds good. Sleep tight.

**Me**: You too.

I sighed all dreamy-like and started to put my phone down on the nightstand, but the text bubble showed up again. I waited. And waited some more. Boring holes into my phone for at least three minutes until finally his message appeared.

**Porter**: Confession: I wish I would have kissed you tonight.

My heart stopped and my stomach dipped as I read it three times before finding the courage to reply.

**Me**: You did.

**Porter**: No. Not like that. I'm talking about one where you'd spend the rest of your night touching your bruised lips, and I'd spend the rest of mine desperately trying to memorize the way you tasted.

My whole body came alive with a hum, from the tips of my fingers to my peaked nipples and everything in between. The sweet ache of arousal. I threw my head back against the pillow and stared up at the ceiling. I'd been with men over the years. After all, sex was just as much about biology as it was about emotion. But, when the orgasm faded, so did my interest in the other person. Looking back on those encounters, I remembered the release—the brief moments when I'd allowed myself to let go and actually feel something with another person. But not once in ten years had I remembered being kissed. I'm positive it had happened, but it hadn't been enough to trigger a memory.

Yet there I was, staring at a text describing a kiss that hadn't happened, but I knew without a shadow of a doubt I'd never forget it.

**Me**: Confession: I wish you would have done that too.
**Porter**: Tomorrow, Charlotte.

It was a promise.
One I had every intention of letting him keep.

---

I spent the morning in the office, catching up on the mountain of paperwork I'd let pile up while I'd been trudging through in the hell of March seventh. I was so behind that it was a wonder I could see over the top of my inbox. By ten thirty, I was still drowning in files, but I could at least see my desk, so I chalked it up as a win and called it a day. The paperwork could wait; Porter would not. Well, I mean, he probably would have, but I didn't want him to. Or, more accurately, I didn't want to have to wait to see *him*.

I'd barely locked the door to the office when my phone started ringing in my hand. Rita's name flashed on the screen, reminding me that I needed to have a nice long chat with her about her taking another stab at the matchmaker game.

"Just the person I need to talk to," I answered.

"And *hello* to you too," she replied in her typical sugary-sweet tone. "What are you up to this fine Sunday morning?"

Wedging the phone between my shoulder and my ear, I opened the door to my car and climbed inside. "Leaving the office."

"Well, that sucks."

"Meh. I'm caught up for the most part. So at least it was productive. Which is more than I'm going to be able to say for the next few days while I'm off burying your body."

"Oh lordy. What did I do this time?"

"Porter Reese," I said pointedly, the mere mention of his name bringing a smile to my face.

The line went silent.

"Shit. Did you talk to him?" she asked.

"Yep."

"And?"

"And I went to dinner with him."

"Oh God," she gasped. "Was he holding you at gunpoint?"

I laughed softly. Then I screwed my eyes shut and dropped my head back against the headrest. "I'm terrified."

"Oh God!" she cried. "Please tell me he didn't really have you at gunpoint."

"No. I was a willing victim. We're having lunch today too."

"Holy shit. Are you feeling okay?"

"Yeah," I replied simply.

But there would be nothing simple about it.

Porter was wrong. I *was* emotionally unavailable. Because letting people in meant risking I'd lose them too.

My fears about dating weren't about the actual act of eating food with someone. It was about lowering my skillfully crafted walls and exposing myself to the elements that raged outside of them.

What if I panicked and couldn't get them back up?

Or what if it only gave reality another chance to ruin me?

But, then again, what if it eased the unwavering hollowness in my chest?

Or what if, at some point over the years, the sun *had* risen again and I'd just been too guarded to see it?

"Holy shit!" Rita exclaimed. "How the hell did he convince you to leave the convent?"

"He's…intense." I bit my lip to stifle a laugh.

And then it died in my throat.

"Does this mean you're going to treat his kid?"

My whole body jerked, and my stomach dropped. Not a dip. Or a flutter. It was an all-out free fall. "I'm sorry. What?"

"I told him you weren't going to do it. But I swear the man wouldn't take no for an answer."

Sweat broke out across my forehead. "His *kid*?"

"Wait…he mentioned this, right?"

"No, he didn't fucking mention this!"

I wasn't stupid; most men my age had children. And, for obvious reasons, it was a deal-breaker. But, then again, there had never been a deal before. At least, not a deal I wanted to keep.

"That piece of shit," she grumbled. "God, why are men such assholes? Oh, right. Because they think with their dicks. Shit…you didn't put out, did you?"

I could barely breathe, much less talk. And, when I didn't say anything, she answered her own question.

"No. No. Of course you didn't."

I gasped for air as I fought the sudden urge to puke. "Why the hell would you set me up with a man who has kids?"

"I didn't set you up with him! Trust me. I learned my lesson about trying to make you happy."

"Then *how* did he find me at the hospital!" I yelled, my traitorous voice breaking at the end.

"Jesus. Calm down. He's been calling the office to get an appointment for his son. I told him you didn't see children, but he was adamant." She lowered her voice. "I felt bad for him, Char. From what I can tell, he's seen every other pulmonologist in a two-hundred-mile radius of the city. He said he'd do anything. So…" She paused, and I could almost imagine her nervously twirling her hair around her finger. "When I found out he owned a restaurant, I told him that, if he catered the Fling, I'd get him a consult with you."

I laughed, but only because it was either that or acknowledge the searing pain in my chest.

Yeah. Porter Reese was amazing.

An amazing fucking liar.

"Did you tell him about Lucas?" I asked, my voice shaking

almost as much as my hands.

She gasped. "Absolutely not. You know I would never—"

"Then how the fuck does he know about the darkness!" I boomed.

It was one lunch, a dinner, three conversations, a chaste kiss on the lips, and then some humorous text exchanges. It was way too soon for my heart to be breaking.

But it was. Wholly and completely.

And not because Porter was a master fucking manipulator.

But because, once again, *hope* had become my greatest enemy.

Hope that I could change.

Hope that I could move on.

Hope that other people like me existed.

Hope that, even if it was only for a few hours, I wouldn't have to be alone anymore.

No questions.

No judgment.

No faking it.

Bullshit. Bullshit. Bullshit.

Forget about the way my nipples had peaked when he'd trailed his callused thumb over my cheek and the way his clean, masculine scent had overwhelmed my senses to the point that it had chased a thrill up my spine. And that heady combination of lust and loneliness that had hung in the air between us until I couldn't decide if I was suffocating or breathing my first breath of fresh air.

My immense physical reaction paled in comparison to the way his *words* had penetrated my mind and stripped me bare.

Porter Reese understood me.

Not in sentences, but in the silence.

Or so I'd thought.

"I have to go," I whispered.

"I swear, Charlotte. I didn't say anything. I figured he'd cater the Fling and you'd tell him no about the kid. No harm, no foul."

With the exception of March seventh, I didn't cry often. Tears were usually spurred by emotion, and I went to great lengths not to feel any of those.

Good. Bad. Happy. Sad.

Numb was always better.

But I'd felt something with Porter. It was small. But, when your entire world was pitch-black, even the tiniest flicker looked like a lighthouse.

Without another word spoken, I ended the call.

Then I started my car and drove home.

All while doing my very best to ignore the twin rivers that dripped from my chin.

# TWELVE

## Porter

SHE NEVER SHOWED FOR LUNCH AT ANTOJITOS.

My mom had the kids, so I sat at that table and waited for over three hours.

I called. They went unanswered.

I texted. She never replied.

I was beyond worried.

Something had to have happened. There was no way she'd been planning to disappear on me. Not after she'd melted into me after dinner, pressing up onto her toes when I'd bent to touch our lips, her breathing labored. She'd been scared out of her fucking mind but clinging to my forearm as though she never wanted to let go.

Yet, as Sunday turned into Monday—and then into Tuesday—it appeared that was exactly what she had done.

I'd spent the weekend with the kids, using every possible distraction to keep my mind off her. But any time I'd laugh or smile, she'd infiltrated my thoughts.

I called again. This time leaving what I hoped was a witty voicemail.

Then, like the true stalker I was starting to fear I was, I texted her again complete with various pictures of Sloth, asking if she was interested in maybe a date with my brother instead. All I got was radio silence.

I told myself to erase her from my mind. It was so absurd that I didn't even know where to start. A few meals and countless smiles didn't constitute a connection. For all I knew, she could have been Catherine all over again. And, if I was being honest, that was what scared me the most.

No. For my own sanity, I had to let it go.

For fuck's sake, I had two children depending on me. I couldn't get lost chasing after a woman. They deserved more than that.

Travis was doing better—temporarily. It happened like that after he got out of the hospital. They'd jacked him up on steroids, giving his fragile body the strength to fight, but within a week, he'd crash back down to baseline, if not lower.

And, because of my insane obsession with Dr. Mills, where I'd asked her to dinner instead of for an appointment for my son, we didn't have a plan for when that happened.

Even knowing that, I *still* couldn't get her off my mind.

Tuesday morning arrived with a bright sunrise. Various shades of orange and peach danced across the horizon as I got the kids up and dressed. And warm rays of sunlight streamed through the windows, forcing me to lower the blinds so Travis could see what his tutor was teaching him. It was a truly beautiful day. Hannah had conned my mom into taking her outside to play on the swing set the moment she'd arrived.

I left for work a few hours later, and as soon as the front door closed behind me, the night fell regardless of the time.

The soft opening of The Tannerhouse was only days away, and we were slammed. Between training the staff, finalizing the menus, and putting the finishing touches on the dining room, there didn't seem to be enough hours in the day.

But, as I sat at a stoplight, staring at the same sign for the interstate as I had every day since we'd bought the building, I couldn't bring myself to take the exit.

I'd told her no questions. But I needed the answer to why she'd stood me up.

Okay, that was a lie.

I just really fucking wanted to see her.

Flipping my blinker on, I merged into the other lane and headed toward her office without the first clue about whether or not she'd actually be there.

Or, worse yet, how she was going to react to my showing up.

Whatever. I could worry about that when I was sure she was okay—and, if I could possibly swing it, wearing one of those secret smiles that spoke to my soul.

Twenty minutes later, I opened the door to North Point Pulmonology.

The gray-haired receptionist slid the glass window open when she saw me approach. "Sign in here, sugar." She pushed a clipboard in my direction.

"Oh, I'm not a patient. I'm here to talk to Dr. Mills."

She scoffed and shook her head. "Sorry, son. Dr. Mills doesn't deal with the pharmaceutical reps. You want a sit-down, you'll have to schedule it through Rita."

"Rita!" I exclaimed a little too loudly before clearing my throat and playing it cool. "Yes. I'd love to talk to Rita. You know...about pharmaceutical stuff."

I pasted on a grin that I prayed came across more endearing than stalker, but I assumed I'd failed when her eyebrows pinched together suspiciously.

"Tell Rita that Porter Reese is here. She'll know who I am."

When she reluctantly picked the phone up, I stole a moment to glance around the office. In my experience, all doctors' offices looked the same. Different furniture. Different magazines. Same sterile environment. While this one was nice and everything seemed new, it still screamed, *Don't get comfortable. Nothing good happens here.* Though that assumption might have been based on my experiences with Travis. It was always bad news with him.

After scanning the large waiting room, I gazed at a display of pictures hanging on the wall closest to the door. Charlotte's name had been engraved on a placard beside a photo of her staring blankly into the camera, the fakest smile I had ever seen pulling at her lips. She was wearing a navy-blue sweater paired with a set of pearls I was positive she hated. Don't ask me how I knew, considering that two of the times I'd seen her she was wearing either an oversized hoodie or a pair of scrubs, but she looked about as comfortable as she would have been in a straitjacket.

I didn't even try to stop the chuckle.

"Don't you dare laugh!" a woman hissed behind me.

I spun and found Rita glaring at me.

"Hey. Sorry to stop by unannounced, but—" I didn't get

to finish my apology before she grabbed my arm and yanked me toward the front door.

"I can't believe you would show your face here after what you did."

I threw the brakes on. "Me? What did I do?"

"Cut the crap and leave," she whisper-yelled before glancing around the waiting room and flashing a placating smile to the two patients watching us.

Confused, I snatched my arm out of her grasp. "I don't know what crap you want me to cut. I'm here to see Charlotte, but the receptionist told me I had to go through you."

She laughed without humor. "You are *not* here to see Charlotte."

"Uh…yeah. I am," I smarted.

Her jaw ticked as she glared at me, and then she exploded into a fury of hisses and angry whispers. "What the hell is wrong with you? You've done enough, okay? Just…leave." She swung a pointed finger at the door.

I narrowed my eyes, a sick sense of unease settling in my stomach. "How about you use actual words here, Rita? What *exactly* do you think I've done to Charlotte?"

She gave me another snarky laugh. "That bullshit dinner? Christ, Porter. I think she actually liked you."

I lowered my voice and shot back, "That's good to hear, because *I* actually like *her*."

She cackled like a bitch. "Right. You want me to believe this has nothing to do with that appointment for your son?"

The hair on the back of my neck stood on end as realization hit me. Planting my hands on my hips, I whispered ominously, "You told her about the appointment?"

"She's my best friend! Of course I told her."

The all-too-familiar anger swirled through me, ricocheting with no way out. Charlotte thought I was after the appointment for Travis…and I was.

But make no mistake about it: I was after her too.

"Where is she?" I growled, closing the distance between us with a menacing step.

All five-foot-nothing of Rita's body went solid, but she pushed up onto her toes to snarl, "Leave her alone. She's been through enough without"—she quieted, but her tone remained threatening—"an *asshole* like you manipulating her. I can't believe—"

I'm sure she kept talking, but I'd heard enough. Charlotte thought I was playing her. The worst of it was that maybe I had been. *Initially.* But not when I'd asked her to dinner. And *definitely* not when I'd asked her to share the darkness with me. And I sure as shit wasn't going to stand there for a second longer while she was somewhere in that office, thinking I had.

Turning on a toe, I stormed toward the door that led deeper into the office and yanked it open.

"You can't go back there!" Rita shouted, but I never slowed.

With heavy steps, I blew through the halls in search of her. I, no doubt, looked like a madman. But that's exactly how I felt. Crazed and irate. I don't know how she did it, but Charlotte eased the ache in my chest. And I'd be damned if I was going to let her walk away without giving me a chance to ease hers too.

A woman at a small desk in the middle of the hallway rose from her chair, panic on her face. "Can I—"

"Dr. Mills," I demanded.

"Uh..." she stammered, but her eyes flashed to the side, giving me the answer long before her mouth ever would.

Following her gaze, I came face-to-face with the saddest eyes I'd ever seen. Her face was blank, but that might have been the most telling part of all. My heart stopped and my lungs burned as realization slammed into me like a Mack truck.

I'd done that to her.

"Charlotte," I whispered in apology.

She was standing at the other end of the hall, her gaze locked on mine, a medical file clutched against her chest, her lips parted in surprise.

Beautiful.

Exhausted.

So fucking broken.

I moved closer. "We need to talk."

She lifted a hand to stop my approach, but she didn't say anything. Her dim eyes stared through me, unreadable and emotionless. She was the distant woman from the Fling, not the vibrant woman from our date. It fucking killed me to see her like that.

"Charlotte," I rasped, inching closer.

"My office," she stated. It wasn't a question or an order. They were just words. Hollow, empty syllables.

*Fuck.*

She moved down the hall in my direction, but she wasn't moving toward me. With careful and intentional steps, she made a wide berth around me.

*Fuck. Fuck. Fuck.*

I'd expected her to be pissed. But this was worse. She hadn't actually said anything yet, but I could tell she'd spent the last two days building that wall of hers taller than ever. Discouraged but determined, I followed her to the door at the end of the hall, preparing a million apologies with every step.

Her office was smaller than I would have expected. The desk was uncluttered, not so much as a Post-it Note in sight. Three bookshelves lined the space behind her desk, all filled with neat rows of books arranged by size, not even a knick-knack to break up the monotony.

Cold and uninviting.

Just like the woman standing before me.

But she was there. Therefore, so was I.

"Talk to me," I pleaded as she sat and motioned for me to do the same.

When I remained on my feet, she sat down and pulled a notepad out of a desk drawer and began writing something down.

"Mr. Reese, Rita told me your son is sick. I took the liberty of calling Patty Rouse to see if she could fit him into their schedule this week."

*Mr. Reese.* My stomach sank. "I didn't ask you out so you'd treat my kid."

She nodded without looking up and continued writing. "I think you'll like Dr. Rouse. Her staff is top-notch."

Positioning myself at the corner of her desk so she couldn't escape—or avoid me—I repeated, "I *didn't* ask you out so you'd treat my kid."

"He'll be in good hands." She finally looked up and smiled, and it was that same fucking smile from her picture in the lobby.

"Don't do that," I breathed.

She intertwined her fingers and, like a true professional, rested them on the desk in front of her.

Cold. Passive. Distant.

She was almost gone. I was losing her to the darkness. And it wasn't one we shared. She wasn't coming back from this one—at least, not for me.

A blast of adrenaline shot through me. "I was going to tell you about Travis at Antojitos."

She blinked. "I have patients waiting. Is there anything else I can do for you, Mr. Reese?"

Propping myself on both of my fists on her desk, I leaned in close. "Yes. Stop calling me Mr. Reese and *talk* to me."

"I'm sorry. I don't treat children," she said, void of all emotion. There wasn't even a flicker of light in her eyes.

Suddenly, frustration roared in my ears. Or maybe it was the same roar of anger that had been screaming inside my head since the day I'd watched Catherine's car land in that river. Both of my children strapped inside.

The same roar that had been deafening me on a daily basis. Only quieting when I had Hannah secured against my side, Travis on my other side, air flowing through his lungs unhindered.

And, as of a few days ago, the same roar she had unknowingly silenced with nothing more than a simple reminder that other people were merely surviving too.

*No questions.*

*No judgments.*

*No faking it.*

*Fuck it.*

I refused to let that go.

Her body turned to stone when I moved in close, curled a hand around the back of her neck, and tilted her head so she was forced to give me her eyes.

"I have no fucking idea what's happening here, but it's not what you think. Do not shut down on me," I demanded.

Her gaze locked on mine. "Step away, Mr. Reese."

"My fucking name is Porter," I boomed, catching her chair and spinning her to face me.

Her eyes flashed with alarm, but she didn't respond with anger the way I so desperately needed her to. Words, I could work with. Chilly despondency, I could not.

Resting my hands on the arms of her chair, I sank to a crouch and balanced in front of her on my toes. We were eye to eye, our bodies a foot apart, but a whole world of assumptions and misunderstandings dividing us.

"I'm going to be real honest here, Charlotte."

"Honesty? From you?" She laughed. "This should be interesting."

I shook my head. "You're hurt. I get it. But that doesn't change my motives. I'm here, right here, right now, for *you*. Not Travis."

"Bullshit." She suddenly rose from the chair, giving me no choice but to move out of her way. With long strides, she began to pace the length of her office, the tail of her white coat floating behind her. "You don't know me! A few quick internet searches and you had me pegged, huh? The poor, damaged woman you assumed you could swoop in and dazzle with your good looks and ridiculous texts." She closed her eyes and laughed. "God, I must have looked like such a fucking fool. All that shit about the darkness, and I bought it wholly and completely. Excellent play, Porter. Bravo." She threw her hands out to the sides before slapping them against her thighs. "Seriously, I'm impressed."

Rising to my full height, I thundered, "It wasn't a fucking play! For fuck's sake, Charlotte, I *didn't* look you up on the internet. I just fucking liked you and wanted to have dinner with you. Sue me, my son is sick and I can't do one goddamn thing to change that except try to get him in with the best doctors that exist. News flash: That's *you*. And yes, I'll admit it, I showed up at the hospital to bring you lunch with every intention of asking you to treat him. But, in true father-of-the-year fashion, I forgot to do it because I was so fucking consumed by *you*." Now, I was the one pacing. "You, Charlotte. Not Dr. Mills. *You*. So say whatever you want. But I swear on my life I have no fucking clue what your deal is." Putting my palm to my heaving chest, I took a step toward her and lowered my voice. "But I don't have to know in order to recognize it. The inferno burns inside me too."

She scoffed and stabbed a finger in my direction. "You have no idea what you're talking about. We don't share an inferno, Porter. You wouldn't last a day in my flames."

A malevolent snarl lifted my lips as a flash of anger ignited me. She was right; I didn't know what I was talking about. But neither did she. I'd promised no questions. But she was about to get a whole hell of a lot of answers.

I closed the distance between us. Her eyes widened as she scrambled away, but I didn't stop until her back hit the wall.

Dropping my elbow to the drywall beside her head, I caged her in with my body.

And then, quick, fast, and to the point, I rained a lifetime of nightmares down on her.

"My wife drove off a bridge with both of my children in the car."

Her whole body jerked, but I kept going.

"I was in the car behind her and got to witness every single horrifying second. So trust me, Charlotte. I'm a fucking expert at the darkness."

"It's not the same," she whispered defiantly.

"I'm not saying it is. All I'm trying to do is tell you *why* I'm here. And why I'm not walking out of this office until you believe me."

After turning her head away, she stared at the blank wall and muttered, "Jesus Christ, say what you need to and then *leave*."

Smirking, I trailed my nose up her smooth neck. Stopping at her ear, I whispered, "Oh, you're coming with me, Charlotte."

Her body remained stiff even as chills pebbled her skin. "Arrogance isn't attractive on you."

I smiled. "Who's lying now?"

"Talk," she snapped.

My lips fell immediately. Clearly, I hadn't thought this through. When she was being dismissive, the truth seemed like the only way to reach her, but now, with her body touching mine, her attitude on full display, I wasn't so sure anymore.

But, if she thought I didn't understand her, I needed her to know exactly how wrong she was.

"Travis was eight and my baby girl was five months old at the time…and that car was sinking with my entire life inside." I paused when the emotion lodged in my throat. "When I got to the car, she was holding Travis." A wave of nausea threatened to knock me on my ass, but I kept talking. "At first, I thought it was protectively, but she wouldn't give him to me. He was frantic, kicking and flailing. And she just wouldn't let him go."

Her gaze snapped to mine, understanding contorting her face. "I don't want to hear this."

I didn't want to relive it, either. I'd told that story exactly one other time: to the police the day of the accident. But, for reasons I'd never be able to explain, it was important to me that *she* heard it.

I sucked in a deep breath that I swear never made it to my lungs. "My adrenaline-riddled mind couldn't figure out what the hell was going on. So I grabbed the back of her shirt and dragged her and Travis out of the window and then went to work on getting Hannah out of her car seat. By the time I hit the surface, my baby's lips were blue. I looked around for Catherine and Travis, but they weren't there, so I had no choice but to pass her off to a stranger who had jumped in after me and went back down in search of them."

Charlotte's hand curled around the back of my neck, and her body came off the wall as she pressed into me. "Stop. I believe you."

I shook my head and stared into her dark-brown eyes, confessing, "I never came back up, Charlotte. At least, not the man I was. That was the exact moment I saw my last ray of daylight." My fingers bit into my palms as I fisted them against the wall, the depths of that river threatening to overtake me all over again.

Her hand cradled the back of my head, her fingers threading into my hair, and our bodies became flush, head to toe. "Stay out of the darkness, Porter."

But there was no turning back. The truth fought to escape, causing my chest to heave, and with each inhale, her body curved around mine as if she were breathing for me. And maybe she was, because I somehow found the air to admit, "She fought me."

Her arms convulsed, and I buried my face in the delicate curve of her neck.

"She'd dragged him back into the car. By the time I got to them, he was passed out and she was barely conscious, but she fucking fought me tooth and nail when I tried to get him out of there. My wife, the woman I'd sworn to love and protect, wanted to die, and she was hell-bent on taking my son with her." My throat closed as the memories overwhelmed me, and my body sagged against hers. "I've never hit a woman in my life, Charlotte. But there was nothing I didn't do to get him from her."

Her fingernails bit into my scalp, the twinge of physical pain doing nothing to distract me from the blast of Catherine's betrayal.

"She was my wife and I loved her. But, as she kicked and hit at me, clinging to the doors while my son floated lifelessly in her arms, the whole fucking car going down with all of us inside, a hate unlike anything I had ever experienced devoured me. Three years later, it *still* roars inside me." Lifting my head, I cupped both sides of her face and rested my forehead on hers. "I was not playing you. I know the darkness, Charlotte. I don't know why it lives inside you, but now, you know why it lives in me."

It started in her eyes, slowly sifted through her features, and then fell down through her body. Brick by brick, her walls crumbled.

"I'm so sorry," she choked out.

I brushed my lips with hers and implored her to believe me, "I *didn't* ask you out so you'd treat my kid. Yes, I hoped it would happen, but that is not the why, okay?"

She nodded, tears filling her eyes. "Did your baby survive?"

"Yeah." I swept my thumbs across her cheeks.

A strangled sigh of relief rushed from her parted lips. "And your wife?"

I swallowed hard and cut my gaze away. "No."

After that, silence fell on the room, but we didn't need any more words. We stood there, her back to the wall, her front plastered to mine, so close that not even the air divided us.

Two people alone in the darkness.

No questions.

No judgments.

No faking it.

Until she decided to turn on the lights.

"Losing your wife doesn't count," she said so quietly that I barely heard her.

"What?" I breathed, sliding my hand around her back and shifting her deeper into my curve.

"You *chose* to love her. You can choose to let her go."

My hand spasmed on her lower back as my head popped up.

Those tears that had been filling her eyes finally spilled out the sides. "I never had a choice, Porter. He came out of me."

My stomach knotted. "I didn't tell you that so you'd open

up. No questions, remember?"

She shook her head. "It was ingrained into me to love him. Morning, noon, and night And then…he was gone." A horrible, soul-searing cry tore from her throat, slamming into me like a physical blow.

I rocked back onto my heels, but not before gathering her impossibly closer.

I held her as though I could put her back together. And, God, did I try as she sobbed in my arms.

"Lucas," she choked out, her tears soaking the front of my shirt. "It was my fault. I left him alone at the park. It was only for a second, and someone took him. It's been almost ten years, and I still don't even know if he's alive or not."

"Oh God," I breathed, pain gripping my chest.

"That kind of love doesn't die, Porter. It grows in the darkness, and I can't make it stop."

"Okay. Okay. Shhh," I urged, my mind barely able to formulate thoughts over the thundering of my heart. "I've got you."

"You don't understand!" she cried, attempting to push me away, but I refused to let her go.

"No. I don't," I assured.

She continued to writhe in my arms, but the way she gripped the back of my shirt made it clear she wasn't trying to get away anymore. "No one fucking understands. The whole world just keeps going on without him. And I can't do it anymore. I can't keep up. I try. And I try. But I can't do it anymore. I need it to stop, Porter."

Cupping the back of her neck, I tucked her face against my shoulder and murmured, "I'll stop with you. I swear to

God, Charlotte. I'll stop with you."

She clung to me with frantic desperation. "I can't treat your son."

I screwed my eyes shut.

Fuck. She really couldn't.

Shame corroded my insides. A part of me had still hoped she would.

But there were other doctors.

And only half of her.

"It's okay," I murmured into her hair.

"I want to. And I swear I would do it for you. But kids and me… We just don't work. They're all him. Every single one of them. Boy or girl, it doesn't matter. They're all *him*."

I rubbed her back. "Shhh…okay."

"I'm so sorry."

"Me too." I tipped my head back to stare at the ceiling. "Fuck. Me too, Charlotte."

She continued to apologize, and I let her because it seemed to soothe her. She didn't owe me those.

We stood there for a long time, our pounding hearts filling the drawn-out silences. Unwilling to sit—or, really, move at all—our bodies swayed as we did our best to balance as a single unit.

She held me.

I held her.

No questions.

No judgments.

No faking it.

But the longer we stood there, the more I realized that those three things were going to be our biggest problems.

With her wrapped securely in my arms, soft admissions pouring from her mouth, reality crashed onto my shoulders like a ton of bricks. I was a single father chasing a woman who couldn't handle being in the presence of a child.

I'd never even had her, yet when she finally stepped out of my arms, I knew I'd lost her all the same.

# THIRTEEN

## Charlotte

I'D NEVER FOR THE REST OF MY LIFE FORGET THOSE MOMENTS in my office with Porter Reese.

The ones where the world finally stopped—even as it kept turning.

I had patients waiting on me, but I couldn't care less. I'd been waiting for over a decade to take a single breath that didn't hurt. And, no matter how much I tried to deny it, nothing hurt with Porter, not even in the darkness.

How Porter gave that to me, I wasn't sure. He didn't understand my situation. But he didn't pretend to. He didn't offer any sage words of advice or try to give me a pep talk about moving on. He just listened and held me.

He'd spoken *words,* I was sure of it. But those moments were all about feelings.

There was something inherently freeing about telling him about Lucas. Our situations were different, but the same shade of black painted both of our souls.

But, as I clung to him, trying to perform the impossible task of collecting myself, it hit me that the darkness was all we'd ever have.

In the light, we lived on polar-opposite ends of the spectrum.

Porter had his children. His future was in ballet recitals and baseball games. And, after hearing his story, I was happy for him. Really, I was. But I couldn't handle being a part of that.

That was his life. Not mine.

And, when he aimed a sad smile at me and used the pads of his thumbs to dry under my eyes, I knew he realized it too.

Leave it to me to connect with a single father. I mean, seriously. Karma was sadistic.

Peering up at him, I softly asked, "So, what now?" I didn't want the answer though.

He shrugged, but it wasn't in indifference. It was disappointment. Heartbreakingly so. It was also real, no matter how much I wished that it weren't.

I sighed. "At the risk of sounding like a teenage girl, I really like you."

His face lit. "I like teenage girls." His eyebrows pinched together as he quickly amended, "Never mind. Ignore that. It sounded way better in my head."

Giggling, I gave him a squeeze.

He groaned as he returned it. "Any chance we can rewind to Saturday night?"

"Would it change anything?"

He tipped his head down so he could see me, his blue

eyes becoming dark and serious. “No. But that doesn’t mean I wouldn’t do it again.”

My stomach fluttered. Jesus, he was such a good guy.

It was going to break me more than I already was to let him go, but I had to end it before I had the chance to beg him to stay.

“Porter, I want to. I just…” I closed my eyes and stepped out of his arms while confessing the one *word* that I feared was starting to dictate my life. “Can’t.”

“I know,” he replied, allowing his fingers to linger on my shoulder until I was out of his reach.

Wrapping one arm around my waist, I attempted to ward off the chill his body had left behind and choked out, “I’m so sorry.”

He twisted his lips—his beautiful, plump, kissable lips. “Don’t apologize. It’s okay. Seriously, I’m not that great. Trust me. You’re getting the good end of the deal.”

I barked a laugh only to start crying all over again. Pointing to my eyes, I said, “This is ridiculous. We barely know each other. You must think I’m insane.”

He chuckled, that deep, masculine sound I loved so much, and it only made the pain in my chest intensify.

“If you’re insane, Charlotte, I’m certifiable. Because this fucking sucks.”

God! The fact that he felt it too made it that much worse.

He brushed the hair off my shoulder, a tingle lighting my skin where his fingers touched. “How about this? If you ever decide you *can*, promise me I’ll be the first to know. I believe I owe you a kiss.”

I fought back a sigh and asked, “How old is your youngest?”

"Creeping on four."

I hiccupped a laugh. "You're in luck. Mills women age really well. I mean, I'm a workaholic who will probably die of a heart attack by the time I'm forty, but if I make it that long, you are in for a real treat."

He smiled and I wanted to cry all over again.

Christ. What the hell was wrong with me?

Oh, right. The first man I'd felt anything with in as long as I could remember was walking out of my life. And I was all but pushing him out the door because he had children.

When he kissed my forehead, I sucked in a sharp breath and allowed a million memories to flash on the backs of my eyelids.

Memories of me laughing, his eyes lit up as he watched me, a huge smile on his face.

Memories of him touching my lips after that kiss he'd promised.

Memories of us curled up on a couch, watching TV together, a fire crackling in the background, but that warmth only he could give me radiating in my chest.

Memories of him making love to me, slow and desperate.

Memories of me coming home to him after a long day's work and crashing into his strong arms seconds before falling asleep.

Memories of us watching the bright sunrise together.

Memories that would never exist.

And then Porter left.

He didn't say anything as he backed out of my office, but goodbyes were spoken all the same. My heart felt as though it were being ripped from my chest with each step he took closer to the door.

He never tore his gaze from mine. It was both a gift and a punishment, because for the first time since I'd met Porter, it gave me the opportunity to see the staggering emptiness in his eyes.

I hated it almost as much as I loved it. He'd lived through hell, but for one lunch, one dinner, and over half an hour in his arms, it had brought him to me.

That was enough.

And, as I watched the door close behind him, I accepted that it would have to be.

It wasn't.

After that day, the sunrise only got darker.

# FOURTEEN

## Charlotte

"Sooo…" Tom drawled.

I set my chopsticks on my empty plate and looked at him, parroting, "Sooo…"

He didn't immediately say anything.

We'd been eating in silence. We did that a lot. It wasn't awkward. Not with us. He was good at the quiet thing, being there and supportive without uttering a word.

Dropping his napkin on his plate, he narrowed his eyes. "How ya doing, Charlotte?"

I shrugged. "Same as every other day."

*Alone. Cold. Hollow.*

He reclined in his chair, but his gaze became scrutinizing. "You seem…off."

I was. I'd been *off* for weeks.

Shaking my head, I lied, "I'm good. Staying busy with work."

He intertwined his fingers before resting them on his stomach. "Your mom says you were dating someone."

I ignored the pang in my stomach at the mention of Porter. Over the last two weeks, I'd done everything I could not to think about Porter Reese. I was good at compartmentalizing. I'd been doing it for years, yet no matter how hard I tried, that man always seemed to weasel into the forefront of my brain.

I was amazed by how many times a day I would stumble across something that would remind me of him.

At first, it was things like dogs, burgers, and cocktail napkins. But it was getting out of control. Now, it was like men, a hand, or, hell, even just a person.

Fine—literally *everything*, including the darkness when I closed my eyes, reminded me of Porter.

I could only imagine the prideful smile that would have split his sexy mouth if he knew how often I thought about him. He would have laughed a deep, throaty chuckle that…

Yeah. I couldn't think about Porter.

But he wasn't even the biggest of my problems.

The day after Porter walked out of my office, I went to the park where Lucas had been abducted. I didn't know why. It had been years since I'd tortured myself with that place. Sitting on that bench, I cried tears from my soul, watching mothers pushing their babies in strollers.

Ten. Fucking. *Years.*

And I hadn't stopped there. After I'd left the park, I'd driven to my old house. The one where my little boy had slept safely, his grunts and coos echoing through the monitor. I'd moved out of that house less than a month after he'd disappeared, but as I stood on the corner, staring at the chipping paint on the blue front door, I called up the memories of the day I'd last walked out of it. And it wasn't the day I'd moved. No. Charlotte Mills had never returned to that house after Lucas was taken.

*I* had—a poor, pitiful excuse for the woman I used to be.

Porter had told me that he'd never reemerged from the water the day of the accident.

I couldn't help but wonder who he'd left behind. And then I wondered if it was possible to get that person back.

Because I desperately needed to find Charlotte Mills again.

By the time I got home that night, I was crying so hard that I threw up. But that didn't stop me from going back the following night.

And the night after that.

*And* the night after that.

Each one ending worse than the last.

Something was seriously wrong with me.

Something worse than Porter Reese.

Something I feared I wasn't going to be able to come back from.

I was losing the only bits and pieces of myself I had left.

"I'm fine," I assured Tom with a smile that I was positive looked no less genuine than it felt. "You and Mom need to stop gossiping like schoolgirls," I added dryly, picking my glass of wine up. (Coincidently, it was the same Sav Blanc Porter had ordered for me at his restaurant. Not so coincidently, I'd specifically ordered it when I had seen it on the menu. See? That guy was *everywhere.*) "Wait…when did you talk to Mom?"

He cut his gaze to the door in the most unlike-Tom way

possible, and I snapped my fingers to bring it back to mine.

"Um…hello? Are you two talking now? Like, on the regular?"

"We're"—he paused, resting his elbows on the table and steepling his fingers under his chin—"worried about you."

I rolled my eyes. "Bullshit. *She's* worried about me. You've seen me at least half a dozen times since my date with Porter and haven't said anything. *You're* worried about *her* being worried about *me*."

The corners of his lip twitched as he confirmed, "And that."

I set the wine back on the table and caught the eye of the waitress, silently asking for a check.

Tom reached across the table and covered his hand with mine.

My heart stopped and somehow exploded all at the same time. It wasn't an odd gesture for Tom. It's just that it was a very *Porter* gesture from Tom.

I snatched my hand away. "I'm fine."

He narrowed his eyes and slanted his head. "See, I'm not thinking you are."

"Okay, well, you're allowed to think whatever you want. But worrying won't change anything. I'm fine. Seriously." I did my best to ignore his scrutinizing gaze by lifting my purse into my lap and digging through my wallet for my credit card.

His voice was rough and pained as he said, "I've been there, Charlotte."

I jerked my head up to look at him. "What?"

He leaned toward me and whispered, "People. We get stuck in a rut and begin to believe the rut is how it's *always* going to be. But it's *not*. You just got to find your way out."

"I went on *one* date with a guy, Tom. We mutually agreed not to see each other anymore. That rut you think I'm in isn't even a divot."

He shook his head and tsked his teeth. "Got my hopes up. Thought you'd finally done it."

"See, this is why I don't tell Mom anything. I go on one date and you two are out shopping for wedding china."

"We saw you," he said, his voice thick with emotion. "Shit, Char. You were smiling and laughing. I have never in my life seen you like that. Your mother burst into tears, cried all over a fifty-dollar steak."

My mouth fell open as I abandoned my search-and-rescue mission for my credit card and set my purse aside. "What are you talking about?" Though it was pretty damn clear. I'd only been to one place recently that served fifty-dollar steaks.

"I finally drew up the courage and asked her out. Managed to swing a late reservation at The Porterhouse. Walked in, your mom on my arm, feeling like a goddamn king. Then we saw *you*." He chuckled. "For the next hour, I paid nearly two hundred dollars on wasted food to spy on you from a booth across the way."

Of course they had seen me with Porter. There were at least a thousand restaurants in the greater Atlanta area. Obviously, they would pick The Porterhouse. Karma wouldn't allow it any other way.

"Fantastic," I deadpanned.

"Yeah, Charlotte. It really was." He stood and pulled his wallet from his back pocket. Then he threw a stack of bills on the table. "You're *not* okay. No fucking way you'll ever convince me of that. Not after I saw that woman at the restaurant."

And then he was gone.

I groaned as he disappeared around the corner.

He was right. I had been okay that night with Porter. I felt it all the way down to my bones. But maybe that was exactly the problem I was having. I'd gotten a taste—the tiniest sampling—of happiness and I couldn't seem to settle back into my life of isolation.

---

I jolted awake at the sound of my cell phone vibrating across my end table. It was dark outside and my body screamed, objecting to the wakeup call. God. How long had I been asleep? It'd been pouring when I'd left the restaurant, so I'd gone home to wait it out before heading up to the park. Though, the second I'd hit my couch, exhaustion had won out.

After snatching my phone up, I pressed it to my ear. "Hel—" I paused to clear my sleep-filled throat and tried again. "Hello."

"Dr. Mills? It's Patty."

I shot straight up, my tired body suddenly coming fully awake as a blast of adrenaline shot through my veins.

"What do you have?" I rushed out, jumping to my feet.

"The transplant team is being called in. Caucasian male. Dilated Cardiomyopathy. A-pos…" She continued to rattle stats off as I tied my long hair into a ponytail.

After sliding my shoes on, I weaved a hurried path through my small apartment and snagged my keys off the bar. "How old?" I snapped, a sharp pain of anticipation piercing me. She didn't immediately answer, so as I attempted to lock the door with shaking hands, I repeated, "How old, Patty?"

*One word.*

"Ten."

My throat closed and I stared at the front door while blinking tears back.

*One word.*

"Lucas," I breathed, rational thought fleeing my system almost as fast as hope filled me.

"Dr. Mills, if I may—" Patty started, but I didn't have the time or the desire to hear her out.

"I'm on my way." I hung up.

The rain poured down in sheets, soaking me to the bone as I jogged to my car. The leather seat of my BMW was cool, but that wasn't why a chill traveled down my spine. I hit his number on my favorites and then lifted my phone to my ear.

"Detective—" he answered, but I didn't let him finish.

Throwing the car into reverse, I yelled, "I found him!"

"Come again?" Tom said.

"I need you to meet me at the hospital. There's a kid," I told him, speeding out of my apartment complex.

"Son of a bitch. I knew it. You aren't all right. Go home, Charlotte. I'll meet you there."

My voice shook as my anxiety grew. "He's ten. Caucasian. Dilated Cardiomyopathy. A-pos. All just like Lucas."

"And just like the last three kids you've dragged me up to the hospital to see over the last ten years. You promised me you'd stop doing this shit."

I had. I'd been managing my hopes well over the last few years. Keeping them so low that they were almost nonexistent. In that time, I'd turned down two middle-of-the-night calls from Patty and the transplant team. Each time, I'd still swing by recovery the next morning, just to be sure it wasn't him. It was never my son though.

But I'd been spiraling out of control over the last few weeks, and I'd actually convinced myself that maybe this time was different.

"This shit is finding my son!" I bit out, gripping the steering wheel tight as I floored it through a yellow light.

"No, Charlotte. This shit is you punishing yourself." He quieted before taking a needle to my bubble of happiness. "It's *not* him."

My frustration flashed to rage. "You don't know that! If Lucas is still out there, he's going to end up on that operating table one day. And goddamn it, Tom, I'm going to be there when he does."

"Sweetheart," he said gently.

I sucked in a deep breath, refusing to allow his negativity to extinguish the only strand of optimism I'd had in years. "It's him," I said resolutely.

"It's not—"

"But what if it is? Isn't it at least worth checking out?"

He laughed without humor. "What are we checking out, Charlotte? A kid? Who is about to get a transplant? You want me to show up there and interrogate his terrified parents? Slap them in a pair of cuffs and haul them down to the station because their son happens to be the same age and blood type as a baby that was taken ten years ago?"

"Yes! That's exactly what I want you to do!" I yelled, knowing how irrational it sounded but completely unable to stop myself.

"Well, it's not going to happen. Everyone in the world with a kid on the donor registry is *not* a suspect."

That was where Tom and I disagreed. As far as I was concerned, they should have been. The cardiac team at the Emory Transplant Center knew me well. I'd called in favor after favor to get the heads-up when a patient matching Lucas's description was brought in. I despised the pity-filled glances they gave me when I'd show up frantic and haggard, but it was well worth it to get those precious phone calls.

I continued to break every traffic law known to man as I merged onto the highway. "Are you coming or not?"

"Don't do this, Charlotte," he said in a low, fatherly warning. "Go home."

"Not until I see him. I'll know if it's Lucas."

His voice grew louder. "Do not go up to that hospital."

"I've got to go, Tom."

"Charlotte!" he shouted, but I ended the call.

Tossing my phone to the seat beside me, I focused on the road. It rang repeatedly during the rest of my drive to the hospital.

With my heart in my throat, I scrambled out of my car and sprinted toward the doors. My stomach was in knots, but I never slowed as I hurried deeper into the hospital, scanning my badge when necessary to get to restricted areas. Nurses spoke as I weaved my way through the hallways, my shoes squeaking against the tile floor with every turn. Excitement and anticipation fueled me forward, my mind reeling with possibilities.

All of them positive.

And all of them ending with me finally waking up from

this nightmare.

But, as I snatched the curtain in pre-op open, I realized that the nightmare was only getting started.

Three pairs of eyes swung my way.

All of them blue.

Two of them matched.

None of them were Lucas's.

I gasped and slapped a hand over my mouth as ten years of pain, hopes, and heartbreak collided, melded together, and then joined forces in a mission to finish me once and for all.

The child's mother rose to her feet, her face filled with concern.

I couldn't begin to imagine what I looked like on the outside, because on the inside, I was a virtual wasteland of despair.

"Are you okay?" she asked.

My glassy eyes flicked to her, my hands shaking and my knees buckling.

*One word.*

"No."

# FIFTEEN

## Porter

"HOW ARE YOU DOING, BABY?" MY MOM ASKED THROUGH the phone.

I rocked back in my office chair and propped my feet up on my desk. "It's been a crazy night. Raul called out, two of the waitresses got into a spat over tips, and we ran out of parsnips."

"Well, all of that sucks, but I asked how *you* were doing, not the restaurant."

How was I doing?

I was functioning. Nothing more. Nothing less.

I smiled on cue, worked more than I would have liked, and obsessed about Charlotte Mills more than I would ever admit.

The minute after I'd gotten home from her office, I'd Googled her.

I'd convinced myself it wasn't a betrayal after she'd told

me about Lucas, but as I'd pored over articles and stared at old photos of her hollow eyes leaving the police station, it had still felt like an invasion of her privacy.

God knew there were dozens of articles about Catherine's "accident," pictures and even videos of me dragging Travis out of the water. I'd have given anything to erase those from the history books, and as I'd shut my computer down that night, I figured Charlotte would probably feel the same way.

I had typed out a million texts to her over the two weeks since I'd seen her—some of them funny, some of them sad, all of them desperate. My conscience hadn't allowed me to send any of them. I refused to be the man who caused her more pain.

And bringing her into my life and then parading Travis and Hannah in front of her would have done just that.

Rita had been right; Charlotte had been through enough.

"I'm fine," I assured. "Tired but fine. Hopefully, I'll be out of here in the next half hour, so you don't have to spend the night if you'd rather wait up until I get there."

"Are you crazy? It's eleven o'clock and raining, Porter. Your father's head would explode if I drove home tonight."

I chuckled. "This is true."

"But," she drawled. "Since I'm stuck here anyway, why don't you go out with Tanner tonight? Maybe hit a disco or something."

"Uh...because I'm thirty-four and it hasn't been called a disco since I was, like, negative ten."

"Oh, hush. Thirty-four is young, honey. Oh, I know! What about that lady you went out with a few weeks ago? Call her and see if she wants to go dancing. Women *love* to dance."

"Mom, stop. I'm tired. I have beyond no desire to go out *dancing* tonight. Or any other night, for that matter. So please, leave it alone."

"Okay, okay. Jeesh. I was only trying to be helpful. You spend all of your time either working or taking care of the kids. You know it's not a crime for you to have a life, Porter."

I groaned. "That's my job, Mom. To work hard so I can afford to take care of the kids and then come home and actually do it."

"You deserve to have some free time in there."

"You're right. I do. But that free time isn't going to be spent going out dancing. It's gonna be spent catching up on much-needed sleep or hitting the grocery store without Hannah begging for the entire cookie aisle."

She sighed. "You know, this might be the only time in your entire life that I'll say this, but it wouldn't kill you to be a little more like Tanner."

I pinched the bridge of my nose and dropped my head against the back of the chair. "Well, if it's that important to you, I'll take my shirt off while I'm cooking the kids breakfast in the morning."

She laughed. "Don't do that. You'll end up with third-degree burns."

I smiled. "Okay. Now, are we done with that?"

"Yeah, I'm done."

"Good. Are the kids asleep?"

"Hannah is, but Trav is sitting here staring at me. I think he wants to talk to you."

"Put him on," I said, sliding my desk drawer open and peering inside as I'd done so many times recently.

Truth was, I would have loved to have a night out, but I would have wanted it to be with Charlotte. Hell, I would have taken her out dancing if that was all I got. Though I could almost picture her horrified expression at the idea of going into a nightclub.

I was chuckling at the thought when his voice came across the line.

"Hey, Dad."

"Hey, bud. Why are you still awake?"

He sucked in a deep breath that sounded like music to my ears. He'd been doing marginally better. Breathing treatments were still a way of life, but he hadn't been back to the hospital, so I chalked it up as progress.

"I've got Minecraft-itis," he said.

I smiled. "That sounds serious."

"It is. And the current treatment plan isn't working. I think it's time to take more aggressive measures and talk to Grandma about giving me back my iPad."

I laughed. "Bud, it's eleven and you have school tomorrow."

His voice remained serious. "No. I have a tutor coming over tomorrow morning. Then I have to spend four hours doing school work. And, by then, I might have wasted away from the effects of this terrible disease. I think we can both agree no one wants that."

My lips lifted in a genuine smile only my boy could give me. "I love you, Travis."

"Is that a yes?" he asked, his voice filled with hope.

"No. Go to bed. I hear Minecraft-itis goes into remission when you sleep. Give it a try and I'll check on you when I get home to make sure your hands haven't turned into pickaxes and your body into diamond armor."

He groaned. "You suck."

"I so, completely do. And you're welcome. Now, go to bed."

I could almost hear him rolling his eyes.

"Fine." He paused. "I love you, Dad."

My heart twisted and grew all at the same time. "I love you too, Trav. More than you will ever know."

My mom came back on the line. "Okay, baby. I'm going to hit the hay now. You be careful driving home."

"I will, and I'll be quiet when I come in. Thanks, Mom."

"No problem. Love you."

"Love you too."

I hung up and reached into the open drawer to pull out that crumbled-up cocktail napkin map.

Yeah. I'd kept it.

Yeah. It made me a bitch.

Yeah. I didn't give a single fuck.

For a few hours, I'd sat at that booth and forgotten about the world outside. I'd listened to a broken woman laughing, and as stupid as it might sound, it had done wonders to soothe the hate inside me.

I traced my fingers over the arrows I'd made leading to the exits, wishing I had taken her hand, dragged her out of that restaurant, and disappeared into the night with her at my side. In that world, outside those doors, Travis wasn't sick, Charlotte wasn't shattered, and I was able to extinguish the fire blazing inside me once and for all. In other words, the impossible.

Closing my eyes, I tossed it back into the drawer.

I was rising to my feet, heading for the door to help the staff finish closing up so we could all get the hell out of there, when I heard the commotion outside.

"I said, wait up front!" Emily, the hostess, called out as my office door swung open.

My whole body locked up tight as a woman came flying inside.

And then my heart stopped, unsure if she was real.

I blinked. Then blinked again. It didn't look like her, but I'd recognize those eyes anywhere.

She was soaking wet from the rain, tears dripping from her eyes, her eye makeup running down her ghostly white face, and her entire body was trembling.

"Charlotte," I rasped, slipping around my desk.

Emily appeared behind her. "I'm sorry, Porter. I asked her to wait out front."

I lifted a hand to cut her off, never tearing my gaze away from the woman I'd somehow willed into fruition. "It's fine. Shut the door behind yourself."

"Yeah. Okay. Sorry," she rushed out, and then I heard the door click.

Alone.

My heart slammed against my ribs and thundered in my ears.

I took a slow step forward, cautious as though the movement might spook her.

She didn't say anything as she stared at me with wild eyes, her chin quivering, her mouth opening and closing as if she were trying to talk.

I curled a finger in the air. "C'mere."

She didn't move, so I stepped closer and kept my voice soft, my arms aching to reach her.

"What's going on, sweetheart?"

She closed her eyes and dropped her chin to her chest, and on a loud sob I could barely make out, she cried, "I need it to stop." She looked back up, the emptiness searing me. "I need it to stop, Porter."

I didn't waste another second. My legs devoured the distance between us until our bodies crashed together, her hand fisting the back of my shirt as she buried her face in my chest.

"It won't stop," she cried, and it was so visceral that it slashed through me. "I just need it to stop."

Gliding a hand up her back and into her hair, I tucked her face into my neck. "Shh… I'll stop with you, Charlotte. I'll stop with you."

She wrapped her arms around my neck and climbed up my body, circling her legs around my hips.

Slapping a hand out to the side, I turned the lights off and plunged the room into darkness—*our darkness*. Then I carried her over to the leather loveseat in the corner and sat with her securely on my lap.

She burrowed into me, her legs on either side of my hips, our chests so tight that I could feel her heart thumping. Strangled words flew from her lips, most of which I couldn't make out. But there was one phrase she kept repeating.

"It has to stop, Porter. It *has* to stop."

I brushed her dripping hair off her shoulder and peppered chaste kisses against her temple, murmuring, "I'll stop with you. Right now, it's just me and you in the dark."

Her body bucked from sobs, and she writhed as though

she were trying to crawl inside me.

I whispered her name over and over, for no other reason than to remind her I was there.

I couldn't be sure how long we sat there, but with every second that passed, the likelihood of letting her go grew smaller and smaller. She was in utter emotional upheaval, but she was in my arms, so I was breathing for the first time in two weeks.

After a few minutes, her chest stopped heaving and her cries fell silent. And a few minutes after that, her tense body relaxed into me.

"There you go," I praised, gathering her wet hair in one hand to get it off her neck.

"It's been ten years. And it's getting worse," she confessed, nuzzling her soft cheek against my stubble.

"No judgments," I whispered.

Her head came up and turned. I couldn't see shit, but I thought I felt her lips sweep mine before she went back to softly nuzzling the other side of my face.

"What's your darkest secret, Porter?"

Without an ounce of hesitation—not with her—I admitted, "I think I killed my wife."

Her body went stiff, and then it melted as if she were somehow relieved.

That time, I *definitely* felt her lips, and my body came alive as she pressed a deep, apologetic kiss to my mouth. I slanted my head, but when I tried to touch my tongue with hers, her mouth shifted to my ear.

"I'm afraid that he's alive," she whispered.

I sucked in a sharp breath and hugged her tight.

"Charlotte..."

Her tone grew painfully intense. "What if whoever took him abuses him? There are horrible people in this world, Porter. What if he's hungry? Would they take him to the doctor when he got sick or just leave him to suffer?"

Those were all serious concerns I couldn't address. But the darkness wasn't about fixing each other. It was only about knowing we weren't alone.

"What if, instead of fighting her, I had forced her to the surface?" I asked. "What if I had realized before that day that she was suicidal? There had to have been clues I missed. I hit her, Charlotte. With the same hands I use to hold my children, I hit their mother and then left her to die." My voice broke as I wrenched my eyes shut.

Her hands framed my face at the same time her lips came back. We both inhaled reverently, sharing the air as though it could bring us closer.

Our parallel conversation continued when she murmured, "For years, I daydreamed about finding him. I must have created a million different scenarios where the police brought him back to me." Her already quiet voice became softer. "Now, I dream about them telling me he's dead so I can finally let go."

Her words hit me like a punch to the gut, my breath breezing over her skin as it flew from my lungs.

I didn't have time to acknowledge the pain because she was waiting for my next confession. And it was probably the darkest one I'd ever have to share.

"For the last two weeks, I've missed you more than I've ever missed her."

She gasped and then whispered a sad, "Porter."

"I get why we can't be together, Charlotte. I swear to God I do. But I've never in my life been able to talk to someone like this. I don't go through the motions with you. For one fucking day, I wasn't numb or angry. But the best part was that you know what it's like, so it wouldn't have mattered if I was." Cupping her jaw, I tilted her head down to rest her forehead on mine. "I know who you are, Charlotte. And I know it doesn't feel like the darkness when we're together." Sliding my hand from her jaw to around her neck, I leaned to the side and lowered her back to the loveseat. "Tell me you feel it too."

Her breathing shuddered. "I feel it."

A heady combination of relief and excitement blasted through me.

She gasped as I followed her down and pressed my lips to her neck. "Oh God," she breathed, threading her fingers into the top of my hair.

I teased my fingers at the waistband of her jeans and trailed my lips to her collarbone. "Any more confessions, Charlotte?" I asked, pushing her shirt up to just below her bra, my hand gliding up the soft skin of her stomach.

I silently cursed the absence of light; she felt fucking beautiful.

"No more confessions," she moaned.

I found her satin-covered breast and rolled my thumb over her peaked nipple, and I said, "Good. Then we're done talking."

Surging up, I took her mouth in a desperate kiss. Her lips opened, inviting me in, and our tongues tangled with greed. A growl rumbled in my throat as she arched up, her soft curves molding around my hard planes.

Never separating our mouths, I planted a knee between her legs on the couch and she shimmied down so the heat of her core pressed against my thigh.

"Fuck," I groaned into her mouth as she circled her hips.

"Please, Porter," she said in a husky voice.

I felt every single consonant and vowel of her plea deep inside my soul. She didn't need to beg. Not now. Not ever. If she wanted anything, I was going to give it to her.

While balancing on a hand on the armrest next to her head, I snaked my other behind her to unhook her bra. Her mouth went to my neck, and her hands never stopped roaming my chest and my back even as she sat up an inch to allow me more space. After fumbling through three tries on the goddamn Fort Knox of bras, I gave up. With hurried movements, I wedged my hand under her hips and jerked her into the sitting position. Then my hands went to the hem of her wet shirt and stripped it over her head. Her bra followed in the same fashion.

I cursed, blindly patting her body down in search of the button on her jeans. It took me approximately ten seconds—and ten seconds too long—to get those off. Her panties hit the floor right behind them.

And then it was my turn.

After catching my shirt at the back of my neck, I tugged it over my head while she went to work with frenzied fingers on my pants. I stood as she struggled to shove them down my thighs, a loud groan rumbling in my chest as her hands purposefully brushed over my shaft.

"Fuck, baby," I mumbled, rolling her nipple in my fingers

as I toed my shoes off and stepped out of my jeans. "Lean back."

With my hand still at her breast, I felt her obey.

I bent, following her forward, and skimmed a finger up her core. Fuck me. She was primed.

"Porter," she breathed, spreading her legs wide, her gentle hands going to my abs as she teetered on the edge of the cushion. That tiny-ass couch wasn't going to work for all the things I wanted to do to her.

Vowing to redecorate my office with a fucking full-size pullout sofa the very next day, I caught her around the waist and lifted her off the loveseat.

She squeaked as I turned and mentally reviewed the horizontal surfaces in my office.

"Fuck," I growled.

"Baby," she purred, circling her arms around my neck as her feet dangled off the hardwood.

"I got a floor and a desk, Charlotte," I announced.

I felt the smile on her lips as she kissed me, long and wet.

"What's it going to be?" I clipped, putting her back on her feet without releasing her.

My hard cock twitched between us, and she glided a delicate hand down my stomach until she brushed the sensitive crown. "Sit down, Porter."

"Char—"

"Sit," she ordered.

I arched an incredulous eyebrow at her demand before realizing she couldn't see it.

After that…I sat my ass down.

She climbed into my lap, getting into the same position

we'd been in when this whole thing had started, only now we were naked and my length was sliding against her slit without ever entering her.

I dropped my head back against the couch as she started a torturous rhythm over me. I gripped her ass, kneading as I urged her down.

After laving her tongue up to my ear, she sucked on my lobe. Then she whispered, "I missed you, too." Her breath hitched before she added, "*So much.*"

I sucked in a sharp breath and my arms tensed around her. Wrapping her up tight, I forced her breasts flat against my chest, and then she blessedly tipped her hips, giving me the access I was desperately searching for.

I entered her on a slow thrust.

"Yes," she hissed, her body stretching around me and hugging my shaft so fucking tight.

Our bodies rolled together as she rode me slow and deep, her fingernails biting into my neck as our moans and groans echoed around the room.

Her teeth nipped. My tongue soothed. Her hands explored every hard curve of my torso, while my hands memorized her soft breasts and her clit.

"Porter," she moaned into my mouth. And then against my neck. And then it became strangled as her muscles clutched my cock as I thrust up hard and rough, forcing her over the edge.

As she pulsed her release around me, her head thrown back, her hair brushing the top of my hand splayed across her back, I could honestly say that it was the most beautiful thing I'd ever seen—and I couldn't even see it.

The never-ending roaring in my ears suddenly went silent as she sagged against me, surrendering her sated body to me and igniting me in ways I had never known possible.

She clung to my neck as I drove into her, harder every time.

"Charlotte," I rasped, burying my face in her neck as my release leveled me.

With the exception of our labored breathing and racing hearts, the room fell silent.

I'd promised her a pretty specific kiss. And, by the time we were done, I knew for a fact her lips were swollen and bruised, and I had etched her taste into every cell of my gray matter.

I also knew there wasn't one fucking thing I wouldn't do to keep her.

# SIXTEEN

## Charlotte

LANGUID AND NAKED, I WAS SITTING IN HIS LAP AS HIS thick cock began to soften inside me. When I'd driven myself to The Porterhouse, desperate for him to stop the world for me, that wasn't at all how I'd thought my night would end. Though, with his arms wrapped protectively around me, his large body flush with mine, his warmth engulfing me even as a chill pebbled my skin, I had not one regret.

He kissed the side of my face and gave me a tight squeeze. "I didn't use a condom."

I tucked my arms between us and wiggled in closer. "I'm on birth control."

"Good," he breathed before kissing me again.

And then Porter did what Porter did best. He made things so charmingly awkward that I couldn't help but feel at ease.

"Just so you know, I've never had sex on this couch before." He paused. "And, honestly, I have no idea why I felt the need to tell you that. But it somehow seemed imperative."

My heart grew at least two sizes in my chest, and not because I was gleeful about the news that I'd been the one to properly christen his couch. But rather because a loud laugh sprang from my throat—the kind that floods you with endorphins to the point of hysterics. And that was exactly what happened as I fell to the side, waves of laughter overtaking me.

And then he joined me.

I'd heard Porter laugh before, but not like that. This one was deep and rich, inherently masculine while still managing to sound boyish and carefree.

"Oh, you think that's funny?" he said, his body folding over on top of me, his hands going to my sides, where he tickled me.

I squealed and flailed against him as he pinned me down, the same fingers that only minutes earlier had been working between my legs with an expert touch now danced over my skin, stirring me into hilarity.

My laugh got louder until tears hit my eyes.

So *this* was what living felt like.

"I can't breathe," I laughed, and his torturous hands finally stopped.

He sat up, and I flipped to my back, draping my legs over his lap. And then those damn multitalented fingers of his went to work, skimming up and down my thighs as we both caught our breath.

"You think anyone heard us having sex?" I asked.

He hummed a sound of approval before adding, "Don't worry. I'll fire them all."

I laughed again, but he didn't join me.

"Charlotte?" he called.

"Yeah, baby?"

"What's going to happen when I turn on the lights?"

My stomach sank. "I honestly don't know."

He slid his hand up until he found mine and then intertwined our fingers. I couldn't make his features out, but I felt his head turn and his gaze come to mine.

"It's still dark outside."

I gave his hand a squeeze. "Then I guess we better make the most of it."

He didn't say another word as he shifted my legs off his lap and pushed to his feet. I watched with rapt attention as his tall silhouette strolled to the door. The faint light from the bottom illuminated him just enough for me to see his hand lift to the switch on the wall.

"It's still dark outside," he repeated. "Artificial light doesn't count."

I grinned. "I'm not going to disappear, Porter."

He sighed. "See, I'm not so sure about that."

And then Porter turned on the lights.

Pain exploded in my eyes as I screwed them shut to allow them time to adjust. After several failed attempts, I finally managed to pry my lids open.

He was still standing across the room, but his eyes were closed and he was shaking his head.

"Porter?" I whispered.

"I fucking knew it." His abs rippled deliciously as he thrust a hand into the top of his hair.

"What?" I asked, sitting up.

His lids opened, heat radiating from his piercing blue eyes as they raked over my body. "I never should have turned that fucking light off." He tipped his chin at me, his lips twitching. "I have a feeling I missed one hell of a show." Then he winked—so fucking sexy.

I bit my lip to stifle the laugh. "The light definitely has its perks." I allowed my gaze to drift down to his toes then back up to his eyes, where I returned his wink. "You are very naked," I said, rising to my feet.

He chuckled. "So are you."

My lips curled up as I prowled toward him, his eyes darkening as I got close.

Stopping in front of him, I rested my hands on his hard chest. "You. Are. Gorgeous."

Folding his arms around my waist, he dipped, touched his lips to mine, and repeated, "So are you."

And then he kissed me, hot and heavy, wiping the smile off my face at the same time that he sent a rush of heat between my thighs.

I pushed up onto my toes to take it deeper, but he lifted his head and ordered, "Put on your pants. You need to clean up, and I don't have a bathroom in here." He released me and went to a closet door behind his desk, his ass gloriously on display as he sauntered away.

I stared unapologetically. He had a *really* nice ass, and it was attached to *really* nice powerful thighs at the bottom and a *really* nice trim and defined back at the top.

It was a fantastic view, and I took full advantage.

"Small?" he asked without turning around.

"Huh?" I asked his ass.

He turned to face me so quickly that I didn't have a chance to divert my gaze.

Aannnnd, now, I was staring at his cock. (I should note that it, too, was *really* nice. Long and thick, even as it hung sated between his legs.)

I jerked my eyes up to his and found him smirking.

My cheeks heated, but I shrugged and pointed at the ceiling. "Sorry. It's the lights."

A huge smile broke across his face. "What size shirt do you wear, sweetheart?"

"Oh. Yeah, small."

He slid a black, neatly folded T-shirt bearing The Porterhouse logo from the bottom of a tall stack and closed the door. His bare feet padded against the wood as he walked back to me.

"Hands up," he said, bunching the fabric together to expose the neck opening. He didn't wait for me to obey before sliding it over my head.

"I need to put my bra on first," I objected.

"It's wet," he said, tugging the shirt down my torso so I was forced to poke my arms through the holes or have them pinned at my sides.

"It'll dry."

He kissed my forehead and snuck a hand between us to pluck my nipple. "And, when it does, you can put it back on."

I gasped and swayed into him, gripping his biceps for balance.

"Come on. Get dressed. I have less than seven hours before the sun comes up. I'm taking you somewhere."

Surprised, I peered up at him. "What? Where?"

He kissed me again and then walked away, muttering, "Somewhere."

I cried a little inside as he pulled his pants on, but then I got to work doing the same. When we were both dressed, he took my hand and led me through the restaurant, to the bathroom. Thankfully, I didn't have to face any of his staff, as it appeared they had finished closing up during our little reunion of sorts.

After I finished doing my business in the bathroom, Porter once again wrapped my hand in his and guided me to the back door, where I waited while he went to the front to lock up and set the alarm.

It was still raining as we ran to his black Tahoe, which was parked beside the back door. He opened my door and I quickly slid inside. Then I giggled as I watched him trying to cover his head as he rounded the hood to the driver's door.

He climbed in, grumbling, "Tomorrow, I'm buying a pull-out couch for my office *and* a fucking umbrella."

I laughed, and he shot me a dazzling smile.

"So, where are we going?" I asked, buckling up then turning sideways in my seat to face him.

A devilish glint danced in his eyes as he announced, "We…are going to steal a car."

I twisted my lips, and my eyebrows pinched together. "Um…why?"

Holding my gaze, he put the truck in reverse and whispered in arrogance, "Because we can." He paused. "And because I'm suddenly feeling seriously inadequate after seeing your BMW parked out front."

I erupted in laughter and followed his gaze as he pivoted

in his seat to see out the back window.

And then my laughter died.

Secured in the center of his backseat was a pink-and-purple flowery car seat. My stomach clenched as I stared at it. An abandoned sippy cup filled the attached cup holder, and a lone Barbie had been haphazardly discarded on the seat beside it.

I wasn't delusional, going through life pretending children didn't exist. I saw them every day. At the grocery store. At restaurants. Riding their bikes in my apartment complex. For the most part, I ignored them. Self-preservation and all.

But that car seat was like the ten-thousand-pound elephant in the room with Porter and me.

Porter's daughter sat in that seat, more than likely singing songs and laughing at her father's corny jokes. His son probably sat beside her, rolling his eyes and acting like he was too cool to hang out with them. All of this while Porter sat in the driver's seat, stealing glances of his babies in the rearview mirror, his heart full and his smile wide.

"Charlotte?" he called, pulling my attention away from the backseat.

I blinked and realized he'd stopped halfway out of the parking spot. Shaking my head, I tried to snap myself out of it, but my gaze kept flicking back to that car seat.

"Look at me," he urged, gently taking my hand in his and resting them both on his thigh. "What's going on?"

I squeezed my eyes shut and squeaked, "It's really bright in here, Porter."

His hand released mine and moved to curl around the back of my neck, at which point he dragged me toward him until our foreheads touched. "Okay. You good with me driving your car?"

I nodded, my forehead rolling against his.

His soft lips came to mine, pressing deep before he said, "Hold on tight, sweetheart."

And hold on I did. It only took about fifteen seconds for him to drive around the building to my car, but I clung to his hand as though he were the only thing keeping me from floating away. I tried not to dash out as soon as he got the car in park, but I suspected I failed, considering I was already in the passenger's seat of my car before Porter had cut the ignition on his truck.

I was silently cursing myself for being such a basket case when he climbed inside and slid the driver's seat all the way back to accommodate his long legs.

Embarrassment assaulted me. "I'm really sorry. I…"

I trailed off when my ass was suddenly up off the leather. My hip bounced off the steering wheel and my legs got tangled on the gearshift, but he didn't stop jostling me until he had my ass in his lap.

"Thirty minutes," he stated matter-of-factly. "I drive an extra *thirty minutes* every day to get to work just so I don't have to go over that bridge again."

My heart soared, and I lifted my eyes to his.

"I'm amending our deal, Charlotte. No questions. No judgment. No faking it." He kissed me and then finished with, "No apologies."

My face got all scrunchy in that hideous way that happens when you're fighting tears back. "You're such an amazing guy."

He grinned. "Does that mean you don't think I'm a serial killer anymore?"

"Not a serial killer, but you proposed grand theft auto, so I'm thinking a life of crime is still a high possibility."

His grin stretched, and he shifted me back into my seat, ordering, "Buckle up, Buttercup."

I followed his directions, and as he pulled out of the parking lot, it was me who was reaching to hold his hand.

# SEVENTEEN

## Charlotte

My mouth fell open as he turned down the long, oak-lined driveway, a huge, white, old-South plantation house appearing on the horizon. It had gorgeous top and bottom wraparound porches that made my mouth water and a brick horseshoe driveway that all but required you to fill it with guests.

"Is this your house?" I breathed, sitting forward in my seat so I could peer up at the extraordinary weeping willows on either side of the house.

He chuckled, lifted my hand to his mouth, and kissed my knuckles. "Sorry to disappoint, but no."

"Then where are we?"

He grinned, releasing my hand to turn my car off. "Somewhere."

"Any chance I'm going to get arrested for being here?" I asked, opening my car door.

On the drive over, the rain had slowed to a drizzle. During those same fifteen minutes, Porter and I hadn't talked much. He'd stolen glances at me out of the corner of his eye, a smile pulling at his lips each time. And I'd clung to his hand, lamenting the moment I had to let it go.

"A small one."

"Fantastic," I deadpanned.

He walked over and hooked an arm around my shoulders, pulling my front into his side. Then he kissed the top of my head. "Relax. It's my brother's house. We aren't going to get arrested, but we are absolutely going to break in." He released me and took my hand, dragging me after him.

I jogged to keep up as he trotted up the front steps. The house was dark, but the front porch light came on when we reached the front door, scaring the shit out of me.

Porter laughed as he dug into his back pocket and pulled his wallet out. "Chill. He's not home. If he were, this whole place would be lit up like Times Square. I swear the man is incapable of turning a light off." He slid a single loose key out and then passed his wallet my way. "Hold this."

I nodded, and as I took the well-worn, brown bifold from his hands, a thought hit me.

The lock clicked, and he stealthily pushed the door open only to stop and stare at me without entering. "Did you take money out of my wallet?"

"Yeah," I answered curtly, shoving a handful of twenty-dollar bills into my back pocket before returning his wallet.

He blinked. "You low on cash?"

I shook my head. "Nope."

He blinked again, his lips beginning to twitch. "So is there a reason you're robbing me?"

"Oh, I'm not robbing you," I said, peering into the semi-open door and glancing around the dark foyer. "I'm taking back what you owe me."

"What I owe you?" he repeated, incredulous.

I had a feeling the house was equally as gorgeous on the inside as it was the outside. I couldn't see much but a stone entryway butted up against dark hardwood floors. The ceilings were high, and I could barely make out a breathtaking split staircase that would have made Scarlett O'Hara froth at the mouth.

Pushing the door wide, completely forgetting I was trespassing, I stepped inside.

"I'm sorry. How exactly do I owe you money?" Porter asked behind me.

"For the upgraded security system," I replied absently, staring at the massive crystal chandelier above us.

His hand hit the small of my back as he got in my space and forced my gaze to his. "I have no idea what you're talking about," he whispered, humor dancing in his eyes.

"After you came barreling into my office a few weeks ago, Greg and Rita insisted we put a lock on the door up front. Now, the receptionist has to buzz you through to the back. It was well over a grand to install, so consider this your down payment."

He barked a laugh and placed his hands on my ass. One slipped into my back pocket, where I felt him retrieve the money. "You forget, sweetheart, you came barreling into my office tonight. And, while I will never in a million years put a security system on my door to keep you out, I'm gonna need that cash to pay to soundproof my office." He nipped my bottom lip.

I kissed him and then mumbled, "Who says I'm coming back?"

His handsome face softened. "I hope like hell you don't ever come to me the way you did tonight. But, if you do, I'll always be there. Door open. Light switch poised. Darkness waiting."

My stomach fluttered and something in the back of my throat prickled. I didn't respond, but I tipped my head back and kissed the underside of his jaw, praying that it somehow conveyed how grateful I was for what he had just given me.

"Come on. I want to show you something." He took my hand, pure Porter, and led me through the dark house, moonlight serving as our only guide to a porch complete with a pair of white rocking chairs and a hammock tied in the corner.

He moved to the swaying ropes and sat before gathering me in his arms and pulling me down on top of him. I went willingly, resting my head on his chest and relishing in his warmth as he wrapped his arms around me.

He pointed over the balcony railing. "There's a pond back there."

I lifted my head to look but couldn't make anything out in the darkness. I settled back on his chest, listening to his heart thumping in my ear, as I said, "This house is gorgeous."

"Tanner bought it about two years ago. I was in a bad place back then." He stopped then amended, "A worse place, anyway. He was worried about me, and I swear to God he never let me out of his sight. He used to come over and sit with me while I stared at the wall, replaying that day in the river over and over, desperately trying to make it change."

I knew that feeling all too well. My lungs burned as I listened to him intently, my hand reflexively twisting in his shirt. He pried it away but only so he could intertwine our fingers.

"You need to understand: I've always loved the water. We grew up tubing and skiing on Lake Lanier with my family. But, after that day with Catherine, I could barely even take a shower without the water slicing through me. It had been over a year, but the hate inside me was getting worse. Well, on a particularly bad day, Tanner dragged me to look at this house he was thinking about buying. I took one look at that pond and lost my fucking mind. Like, I'm not kidding, Charlotte. *Lost. It.* It was beyond freezing, but fully clothed, without even emptying my pockets, I ran into that pond, cussing and screaming, slamming my fists against the surface as if I could hurt the water as much as it had hurt me." He swallowed hard. "I needed the pain to stop in a bad way."

Tears were in my eyes as I curved my body into his side. I hated how much Porter and I shared. At the same time, it filled me in unimaginable ways.

"That was me tonight," I confessed.

He nodded, acknowledging my words, but he didn't let it veer him from his story. "Tanner followed me in. Floating beside me on his back while I lost my shit. When I'd finally exhausted myself, we were both shivering uncontrollably and he forced me to the shore, where we collapsed on the ground. Staring up at the sky, I asked him, 'What the hell is wrong with me?' And my dumbass, clueless, little brother, whose greatest difficulty in life had been deciding what woman to sleep with on Friday night, looked at me and said the most profound thing I had ever heard. 'You're done holding on, Porter. But you have no fucking idea how to let go.'"

I gasped and my body turned to stone as the words permeated through me. That was exactly how I felt. Like I was hanging on the edge of a cliff, my fingers slipping, my aching and exhausted body dangling above the promise of a future, while my little boy's dark-brown eyes stared at me from above. How was I supposed to make a choice like that?

"Porter," I breathed. "I don't know how to let go of him."

His fingers sifted through the back of my hair, and he pressed his lips to my forehead and whispered, "Nobody does, Charlotte. I *still* don't. But Tanner bought this house, and every summer, the minute it gets warm enough, I walk into that pond and *try* to learn."

My breathing shuddered as I found the courage to tell him, "I've been going back to the park where he was taken."

He kissed my head again, allowing his lips to linger as I kept talking.

"It's like I'm waiting for a sign that it's okay for me to let go."

He tipped his head down to catch my gaze and asked, "You seen anything?"

"I see *you*," I choked, the tears finally slipping from my eyes.

His hand flexed at the back of my head. "Charlotte."

"I don't want to watch you walk away again, Porter. Can you give me some time? A few days, a week or so tops, just to get my head on straight? I'm not saying I'll be better and this thing between us will work. But I really want to try."

His warm palm came to my face. "Sweetheart, I'll give you fifty years if you need it."

I half laughed, half cried. "Okay, don't get crazy. Mills women don't age *that* well."

Porter didn't laugh. He kissed me.

Apologetic and reassuring.

Deep and meaningful.

Heartbreaking even as it eased me.

It was unlike anything I'd ever experienced.

Porter kissed me with hope.

And he didn't stop even as I guided his hand down between my legs.

Nor did he stop as he lowered me to the wood slats on that gorgeous wraparound porch, slowly sliding my jeans off before pushing inside me.

I cried into his mouth, moans of pleasure and sadness as his hard body moved over me, waves of ecstasy colliding with the weight of gravity that had me pinned to the Earth.

And then he kept kissing me, the sweet taste of his hope tingling on the tip of my tongue long after we'd both found our releases.

Porter and I never left the porch that night.

We took turns going into the house. Me to use the restroom, him to grab a couple of beers. But, even with as beautiful as that house was, the porch was infinitely better.

We dozed in the hammock, waking up only to kiss or gather each other closer before falling back asleep.

At exactly 6:17 that morning, while held tight against Porter's chest, his pouty lips parted in slumber, my head rising and falling with his even breaths, his warmth enveloping me inside and out, my eyes aimed at the horizon, I saw my very first sunrise in almost ten years.

# EIGHTEEN

## Porter

"DADDY!" HANNAH YELLED FROM THE OTHER SIDE OF the door as I stepped out of the shower. "Travis stole my charger!"

"I did not! This one is mine!" he argued behind her.

"Nuh uh!" Hanna returned.

"Ya huh!"

"Give it to me!"

I stared at myself in the mirror, a small smile lifting the side of my mouth, and tied the towel around my hips.

Yep. That was my life. And, as frustrating as it could be sometimes, I fucking loved every second of it.

It had been five days since I'd watched Charlotte drive out of The Porterhouse parking lot after she'd dropped me back off at my car. She hadn't called or texted in that time, but I knew she would when she was ready. Whenever that might be. I didn't have the first clue how the two of us would ever make something work. But, if she was willing to try, so was I.

It wasn't like I was in a huge rush for her to meet my kids. After everything they had been through, introducing them to a new woman in my life was a long way off. We could take it slow, learn to let our pasts go together before starting a future. Even if that was only phone calls and texts, late-night dinners after the kids went to bed, and maybe the occasional overnight at her place when my Mom could watch them. I just wanted Charlotte. Any way I could have her.

"Stop! You're going to break it!" Travis shouted.

"Let go!"

"No, you let go!"

Careful to tuck my smile away, I yanked the door open. "Would you two stop fighting?"

Travis kept his gaze on his sister, one hand clenched around his iPad, the other tugging at the end of a white charger. "This one's mine!"

I pulled the cord from between their warring hands. "Well, now, it's mine."

"Dad!" Travis whined. "I only have eight percent left on my iPad. It's going to die."

"I only have fifty-eleven percent left," Hannah cried behind him, clearly needing to get back into preschool.

I sucked my lips between my teeth and bit down to stifle a laugh. Then I headed for my bedroom door, ordering, "Out. Both of you."

"But, Dad—" they whined in unison.

I cut them off. "You don't need to be on your iPad anyway. Travis, go get ready for your tutor. We can hash out chargers this afternoon. *After* you finish your schoolwork. And,

Hannah, go get dressed. Grandma's busy this morning, so you're going to The Tannerhouse with me."

Her eyes lit. "Is Uncle Tan gonna be there?"

I smiled. My girl did love her uncle. "Maybe. Hurry up and get out of here and I'll text him to find out."

"Woohoo!" she cheered, skipping out of my room.

Travis followed her, grumbling, "It was my charger, Hannie."

"It was not!" she screeched.

"Hey!" I barked. "I said stop fighting!"

I shut my door and got dressed, strategically avoiding the picture of Catherine on my dresser. Then I headed to the kitchen to throw some frozen waffles into the toaster for the kids—okay and me too. Those things were fucking delicious. I spent an extra thirty minutes a day at the gym working those babies off.

Hannah came prancing into the room wearing a hot-pink-and-white-zebra-striped shirt and green-and-black-polka-dot leggings that clashed so loudly that it was almost deafening. Her long, curly hair was a rat's nest, and her rain galoshes were on the wrong feet.

I smiled.

She smiled back and then climbed onto her stool at the bar.

"Travis, breakfast!" I called, cutting her waffles up as my cell started ringing.

My boy came wandering into the room, wearing basketball shorts, a T-shirt, and a pissed-off scowl on his face.

I lifted the phone to my ear. "Hello?"

"Mr. Reese?" a woman said.

"You got him." I slid a plate in front of Hannah and then turned to grab one for Travis.

"Hi. I'm calling from Dr. Mills's office at North Point Pulmonology."

I froze at the mention of her name. "What can I, uh, do for you?"

"Dr. Mills asked me to call and see if you would be able to bring Travis into the office this morning?"

I dropped the plate on the counter with a loud clatter and nervously switched the phone to my other hand. "I'm sorry. Come again?"

"Your son, Travis. We were hoping you could—"

"Charlotte asked you to call me?" I clarified.

"Yes, sir. She—"

Hope blasted through my veins, but it was iced by immediate concern. "And you're positive she wants me to bring my son?"

"That's what she said."

I blinked several times and then glanced up to Travis, who was sitting at the counter. His face was pale, his eyes sunken from exhaustion. We'd managed to keep him out of the hospital, but that didn't mean he was doing any better. We'd been up three times last night doing breathing treatments. After the one at five a.m., I hadn't bothered going back to sleep.

There was nothing I wouldn't have given to get him the help he so desperately needed, but not at the risk of destroying her. She'd struggled when she'd seen Hannah's car seat in my car, and now, five days later, she was going to treat my kid?

"I can't," I said, bile crawling up the back of my throat. I stood there, rooted in place, my hand gripping the back of my neck, as I stared at my children, who were once again fighting over God only knew what.

They depended on me. *He* depended on me.

It was my job to make the hard decisions and my job to put them first no matter the cost.

She'd decided to treat him—for me.

But I knew exactly how it was going to gut her. I felt it every time I thought about that bridge.

Then again, if she thought she could do it, who was I to argue?

Oh, right. The man who was going to have to watch the woman he cared about crumble if and when she realized she couldn't.

Indecision warred inside me, spiking my pulse and sending a flurry of memories racing through my mind.

*"I need it to stop, Porter."*

*"Daddy, he can't breathe."*

*"Every single one of them. Boy or girl, it doesn't matter. They're all him."*

*"Who's going to take care of me now?"*

*"I don't know how to let go of him."*

But, at the end of the day, there was only one choice.

*"I love you, Dad."*

"Okay. I'll let Dr. Mills know. Have a great day, Mr.—"

"Wait!" I shouted, causing the kids to snap their attention to me. Their brown eyes bored into me as I sucked in a ragged breath. "We'll be there."

---

My heart was in my throat as I walked up to the front door of her office with Hannah on my hip, her shoes still on the wrong feet, and Travis hot on my heels, his palm wrapped in mine.

I'd texted Charlotte seventeen times since I'd hung up with her nurse who'd called me.

She'd replied exactly zero times.

The strangest mixture of guilt and elation swirled in my chest as I walked to the reception desk.

The sound of her broken voice telling me, "I can't treat your son, Porter," played on a continuous loop in my head, creating something of a soundtrack for the visual of Travis sitting on the side of the tub, a nebulizer between his lips, tears dripping from his chin.

I was doing the right thing. I knew it to the core of my soul. But that didn't mean it didn't fucking burn like the hottest flames, knowing I was doing it to *her.*

The same gray-haired receptionist slipped the window open as we approached, her wrinkled glower leveled on me. "Mr. Reese. We meet again." She rose from her chair, pointedly reached across the desk, and pressed a buzzer. "Come on back. We've been expecting you."

I nodded and swallowed hard. "Look, is there any chance I could see Charlotte for a minute alone before I bring the kids back?"

Rita suddenly appeared in the doorway. Her gaze slipped to Travis then to Hannah before finally meeting mine. "Come on, Porter. Charlotte's in with a patient."

"Rita," I called, shifting Hannah to my other hip and reaching to grab Travis's hand again. "I need to see her first."

She gave me her back as she guided us down the familiar hallway.

"Rita," I hissed. "I need—"

She abruptly stopped, which caused me to bump into her back. Her pretty face was hard as she turned to me, but her eyes were soft. She flashed her gaze to Travis and offered him a genuine smile before pinning me with a glare and whispering, "If you hurt her, I will kill you."

"I'm not trying to hurt her. I'm trying to—" I whisper-yelled but she shoved the door at her left open and walked inside, leaving it wide for me to follow.

I made it exactly two steps inside before I froze.

Three doctors in white coats all rose from their seats behind the long conference table.

None of them were Charlotte.

One I vaguely recognized as Dr. Laughlin from his picture hanging beside Charlotte's in the waiting room, but I'd never seen the two older women before.

"You must be Travis," a thin woman with chin-length salt-and-pepper hair said as she approached, her hand extended toward him, a warm smile pulling at her lips.

Travis peered up at me skeptically before accepting her hand. "Hi."

"Hi. I'm Dr. Gina Whitehall. I came a long way to see you." She winked then craned her head back to look up at me. "I'm so glad you could make it, Porter."

"Yeah, me too," I said absently, confusion ringing in my ears. "Where's Charlotte?"

"She's with a patient. But she's not going to be joining us today," Dr. Laughlin stated gruffly.

I blinked and scanned the room. "Okay. So, why are we here then?"

"I have to pee," Hannah whispered in my ear before anyone could answer me.

"I'll take her," Rita offered. "I mean…if that's okay with you? I think I've got some crayons in my office. We could hang out until you guys finish up here."

I cut my gaze to hers and whispered, "What's going on?"

She smiled tightly. "Just sit down and listen, Porter. And I'll repeat: If you hurt her, I *will* kill you." She clapped her hands together and extended them toward Hannah. "Come on, honey. Let's go get a snack."

I did another sweep of the room, more puzzled than ever.

"Go ahead, baby. I'll be right there," I said, passing Hannah off to Rita.

When my arm fell to my side, Travis took my hand and pressed into my side. I glanced down and found him staring up at me, anxiety painting his face.

"It's okay, bud," I assured even though I had no idea what the hell was going on.

"Travis," the other, slightly round, woman greeted warmly. "I'm Dr. Erin Hoffman, the head of pediatric pulmonology at Texas Children's Hospital. You can relax. We're only here to talk to you today." Her smile lifted to me. "Have a seat, Porter."

I couldn't have moved if the Earth had suddenly caught fire. "I'm sorry. Did you say you're from Texas Children's Hospital?"

Dr. Hoffman chuckled. "So you've heard of us."

We lived in Georgia, but I knew all about TCH. When your kid was sick, you made it your job to know who the best doctors were. And, while Charlotte seemed to be Atlanta's best, TCH was the country's best. They were the people you sold your soul to get an appointment with.

And here they were. Halfway across the country. To see my son.

The oxygen in the room suddenly disappeared and the ground beneath my feet rumbled.

"How?" I asked, reaching down to balance myself on the back of one of the chairs.

Dr. Whitehall smiled and shrugged. "Charlotte Mills is a good friend and an even better doctor. She asks you to come see a patient, you come see a patient. Who knows when you'll need her to return the favor."

And, just like that, the brightest light I had ever seen illuminated the darkness.

# NINETEEN

## Charlotte

I'D WATCHED THROUGH MY OFFICE WINDOW AS PORTER arrived. I'd felt like a masochist unable to look away as he'd guided his children up the sidewalk toward the door.

His little girl was beautiful. She looked just like her father, but with a darker complexion. The hole in my heart stretched painfully as she lifted her hands in the air, asking for him to pick her up, an offer he accepted without hesitation. He had a certain practiced ease about it as he fluidly lifted her off the ground and planted her on his hip, her silly rain boots brushing his thigh.

And then there was his son. It felt like a knife to the chest as I watched him intently staring up at his father, his pouty lips moving with questions, Porter's matching set moving with replies. He didn't have his dad's strong jaw or broad shoulders; those would surely come with age. He did, however, have his father's mannerisms, especially the one where he grabbed

Porter's hand as they walked. Travis was pale and thin, his hollow cheeks and sunken eyes worrying me immediately.

But he was there, and so were Dr. Hoffman and Dr. Whitehall.

I'd done all I could do for that little boy.

Letting the curtain fall back into place when they'd moved out of sight, I ambled to my desk, my chest empty and my throat burning. But there was the tiniest seed of hope sprouting in my stomach.

I'd stayed hidden in my office until I'd gotten the all clear message from Rita, letting me know Porter and Travis were in the conference room. And only then did I allow myself to open the thread of texts Porter had sent me that morning.

**Porter**: You don't have to do this.

**Porter**: Charlotte, please talk to me. I can't bring him up there unless you let me know where your head is at.

**Porter**: You have to say something or I'm not coming.

**Porter**: Goddamn it, Charlotte. Answer me.

**Porter**: I'm on my way. And I'm fucking terrified this is going to break you.

My throat was thick with emotion as I continued reading the rest, each one a similar variation of the last. He was worried about me, a thought that warmed me.

I hadn't trusted myself to read those texts when they'd been buzzing in my pocket. I might have been tempted to reply, and there was no way Porter would have agreed to come if he had known how anxious I truly was about that morning.

In the days since I'd last seen Porter, I still hadn't figured out the magic I needed to reclaim my life in the light, but I had decided to try. One finger at a time, I was going to let that cliff go. How could I not? Porter was waiting for me at the bottom.

Stashing my phone in my pocket, I headed to the door. My schedule was slammed on Mondays, and I was already behind. And, when I pulled my door open, I knew I was going to run a whole lot later.

Porter was standing there, looming in the doorway. His jaw hard, the veins on his neck straining, and his gaze dark—like scary dark.

"What did you do?" he accused.

My chin jerked to the side.

Was he pissed?

"Uh," I stalled, rocking back onto my heels, giving myself time to formulate a response.

His Adam's apple bobbed in his throat, and then he repeated, "*What* did you do?"

Holy shit. He *was* mad.

My mouth fell open as a herd of angry bumble bees roared to life in my stomach. "I…I told you I can't treat him."

His eyebrows pinched together as he scoffed. "So you decided to fly in two of the best pediatric pulmonologists in the entire fucking country on five days' notice without

talking to me first?"

Squaring my shoulders, I fearlessly held his angry gaze. "Well…yeah. Just because I can't treat him doesn't mean I don't want him to get the best care possible."

And that was when I hit the brick wall. Or, more accurately, Porter's hard body slammed into mine. One hand fisted into the back of my hair, the other looping around my hips as he lifted me off my feet and stormed into my office with me dangling in his arms. He must have kicked the door shut, because it slammed with a loud crack.

Breath flew from my lungs when my back roughly met the wall, Porter's chest hitting mine, his hips pinning me, and his hands showing the slightest of trembles.

Only then did I realize Porter wasn't angry at all.

He was completely and utterly overwhelmed.

Circling my arms around his neck, I kissed the side of his face and whispered, "Baby."

"They're taking him as a patient," he stated, his voice breaking as he tucked his face in my neck.

I swirled my fingers in the short hair at the nape of his neck. "Laughlin is going be his primary, but Whitehall is going to be writing the orders remotely."

His shoulders gave the softest of shakes. "They're gonna treat my boy, Charlotte."

My heart splintered as I clung to him tighter. "They are. And they're amazing doctors."

"Jesus," he cursed, his shaking fingers biting into the back of my head. "I can't repay you for this."

I kissed his face again. "You make the world stop, Porter. This was the least I could do."

He shifted his body, bringing himself closer, but he never looked up. "Are you done getting your head straight?"

"No," I admitted.

He nodded. "You ready to let me help you do that yet?"

I closed my eyes and breathed, "Porter. I don't—"

His deep and masculine voice became desperate. "Let me in, Charlotte. We'll take it slow and start in the dark if that's what you need. But I want you in the light, sweetheart. Whatever it takes to get you there, I'll do it. I just need you to let me in so I can try." His head popped up, and his eyes blazed with emotion, but it was his lips, not his *words*, that translated it.

A shiver ran down my spine as he kissed me with earth-shaking reverence.

"I missed you," I confessed against his lips.

"We don't have to miss each other. Just let me in," he pleaded before another kiss.

My lungs constricted and my heart swelled. He had a point. We *could* take it slow. I'd been sitting still as the world had spun around me for ten years. There was no rule stating that we had to jump in feet first. Maybe a quiet stroll, where we both eased into the light, was exactly what we needed.

And this was Porter. I wouldn't mind the extra time spent growing things with him because he'd be there with me every agonizing baby step along the way.

I was still clinging to his neck when I felt the first of my fingers slip off that cliff.

And it was only that split second of realization that made me say, "Okay, baby."

All at once, he pulled away from my mouth and set me on my feet. The tip of his finger traced my hairline as he tucked a tendril of hair behind my ear, and then he rested his forehead against mine. "Tonight. I'm coming over to your place. It's going to be late and I can't stay long, but I'm not waiting a single night longer to start this with you."

I nipped at his bottom lip. "I'll text you the address."

He smiled a classic Porter Reese heart-stopper, pecked

me on the forehead, and released me.

And then he immediately took my hand and intertwined our fingers.

His warmth flooded my system, and I giggled as he guided me to the door.

"What's so funny?" he asked, his hand poised on the knob.

I lifted our braided fingers in the air. "It's just you really have a thing for holding hands."

He arched an eyebrow. "Does that bother you?"

"No. Not at all. I mean, it kinda freaked me out at first, but I like it now. It's you."

He smirked and tugged on our joined hands, forcing me against his chest as he held them behind his back. Tipping his head down, he brushed his lips with mine. "You're hard to read, Charlotte. But your hands always tell me the truth." His voice got low and husky. "You grip me tight when you're nervous or anxious. You squeeze me soft when you're being sweet. And you pull it away when you're trying to hide." He nuzzled his face with mine and breathed, "Tonight, we'll figure out what your hands do when I'm making you come."

"Jesus, Porter," I exhaled and gripped his hand tight.

He moved our linked hands from behind his back and lifted them in the air, pointedly tipping his chin at my death grip. "I'm going to assume that's what they do when you're turned on."

I laughed and shook my head. "Courtesy FYI: It's still not attractive when you're arrogant."

He grinned, well…arrogantly. "I see you're still lying to yourself."

I rolled my eyes, but I was helpless to stop the laugh that

erupted from my mouth.

His smile grew as he pulled the door open and stepped into the hall. With his heated gaze anchored on mine, he stretched his arm long and held on to me until the distance between us forced him to let go.

*So. Fucking. Porter.*

I moved to the doorway and propped my shoulder on the jamb to enjoy the show of him walking away.

And then my heart stilled when I saw Rita standing at the nurses' desk, Hannah on her left, Travis on her right, her apology-filled gaze locked on me.

I sucked in a sharp breath as I watched Porter hurry to them. He hooked them both around their necks before hugging them to his thighs, saying, "All right, pipsqueaks. Let's get out of here."

Instinct told me to turn away. But I stared, unable to stop myself.

Hannah giggled at her father, while Travis fought a smile and spun out of Porter's hold.

"Dad, stop," he complained. Suddenly, his dark eyes landed on mine and my whole body jerked at having been caught.

"Hi," he said, lifting his hand for a finger wave.

My stomach rolled, but I somehow managed to return the gesture.

Porter's gaze snapped to mine, concern so heavy in his eyes that I felt the weight of it sweep over me.

"Trav, lead the way out," he ordered, and the kids took off, but Porter came straight to me.

"I'm okay," I assured, forcing a smile, before he could get a word out.

He cupped my jaw, his thumb gliding across my curved lips as he scolded, "Rule number three, sweetheart."

*No faking it.*

I covered my hand with his and turned into it so I could kiss his palm. "Rule number two, Porter."

*No judgments.*

He sighed and dropped his hand. Bending forward to touch his lips to my hair, he murmured, "Tonight."

My stomach fluttered as I nodded and whispered, "I'll leave the light off for you."

With one last smile and a wink, he took off, his long legs stretching to catch up with his kids.

And then he was gone.

*Until tonight.*

---

"Come on, Charlotte," Porter growled into my ear.

My hands were pinned over my head, our fingers laced together, and my legs were wide as he drove into me, hard and fast.

"I'm close, baby," I panted.

Porter hadn't even said hello when he'd arrived at my apartment that night. That is unless you counted him stripping my bra off (again, over my head) and latching his hungry mouth over my nipple. In which case, it was quite possibly the best hello anyone had ever given me.

His talented fingers had been in my panties before I'd managed to get his shirt off.

Though, I assumed this was what you got when you answered the front door at eleven thirty at night in nothing but a few scraps of black lace and a pair of heels that even I had to admit were sexy as hell. This setup had required another trip to the mall after work, another blowout at the hair salon, and, yes, another trip past the MAC counter. But, given Porter's reaction, it was worth every penny.

I had come on his hand before we'd even made it out of my living room.

And then I'd come again on his mouth before we'd even made it to the bed.

And, now, I was about to come on his cock, thankfully on a soft mattress, but that was about the only thing soft about it.

My cheeks were raw from the scruff on his jaw, and my breasts were tender from his constant attention.

While we both liked the darkness, that wasn't an option for Porter that night. My apartment probably looked like an airport runway leading to the bedroom. As we'd banged into walls and knocked over the few picture frames that decorated my apartment, Porter had turned on every single light he could find.

He was a gorgeous man, so I did *not* complain about getting to watch his abs ripple as he rolled his hips with every thrust. Nor did I complain about the view of his back tensing as he feasted between my legs. And I sure as hell wasn't about to complain about getting to witness the indescribable beauty of Porter Reese losing himself inside me.

"So fucking perfect," he growled, planting himself to the hilt, his gaze so heated that it caused the cool air to pebble my skin. After releasing my hands, he hooked his arm under the backs of my knees and pressed them high.

He slid deep, and I moaned as my orgasm tore through

me. My whole body convulsed. Toes curling, stomach tightening, core clenching, fingers tingling, breath shuddering.

"There we go," he praised as his pace quickened.

I was still floating through my high when I felt his body tense and a strained whisper vaguely sounding like my name breezed from his lips.

*Seriously fucking beautiful.*

He lowered my legs back to the bed, and his body sagged as he rode his release out inside me.

I lay there, beneath his heavy but incredibly comforting weight, silently trailing my fingers up and down his back for some time.

Just when I was starting to believe he had fallen asleep, his head popped up and a gentle smile pulled at his lips. "Hi."

I grinned. "Hello to you too."

He dipped low and kissed my lips before rolling off me, but he didn't go far. Propping his elbow on the bed, he cradled his head in his hand and stared at me. "You always answer your door in lingerie?"

"Of course," I answered, rolling to my side to face him. "I find it bolsters the neighborhood morale."

His lips twitched. "It sure as hell bolstered mine."

I laughed and scooted closer.

He took the hint and shifted to his back, stretching his arm out so I could rest my head on it and curl into his side.

"How was the rest of your day?" he asked the ceiling.

"Busy. I spent two hours playing catchup with patients. Sent one up to the hospital. Then I had an early dinner with Gina and Erin before they had to catch a flight back to Texas."

His arms spasmed around me, and his lips found my

forehead, where he murmured, “You’re amazing.”

“Not really. It was Japanese, my favorite. So not exactly a sacrifice.”

He chuckled. “You know what I mean.”

I draped my arm over his stomach and gave him a squeeze in acknowledgement. “How long can you stay?” I asked.

He groaned. “Not long. I told my mom I’d be home by twelve thirty.”

“Ah, curfew,” I teased, doing my best to keep the sadness out of my voice. What I wouldn’t have given to fall asleep in his arms like we had that night on the porch at his brother’s house.

“I have to be at The Tannerhouse tomorrow night until nine. I’ll be busy, but why don’t you and your girlfriends come by and have drinks?”

“I have one girlfriend, Porter.”

“Okay, so you and *one* girlfriend come by and have drinks on the house. I’ll drive you both home after.”

I smiled and tipped my head back to peer up at him. “Is there a couch in your office there too?”

“Yes. But Tanner uses that office more than I do, so you’d have to be wearing a hazmat suit before I’d ever allow you to sit on it.”

I laughed, and God, it felt so freaking good. It was my favorite part of the Porter Reese effect. “I wish I could, but I’m on call tomorrow night. What about Wednesday night?”

He groaned. “Can’t. I’m off on Wednesday.”

Normally, this would have been good news. I didn’t have office hours on Wednesdays, so barring any emergencies, we could have spent the day together.

But I knew exactly what Porter's being *off* meant. He'd be spending the day with his children.

"Oh," I breathed, my disappointment obvious.

"What about lunch on Thursday? I have a manager on vacation, but I don't have to go in until three."

I smiled tightly. "I have patients on Thursdays."

His lips thinned, his frustration matching my own.

"It's okay," I told him. "We'll get together this weekend or something."

He sighed and folded his arm under his head. "I'm off this Friday too because I have to work both Saturday and Sunday nights."

I didn't say anything else as I cut my gaze away and began staring at the wall.

Apparently, this whole dating-a-single-dad thing was going to be a lot more difficult than I'd thought. And that sucked something fierce because I loved spending time with him, even if it was silently in the darkness. Just knowing that Porter was there freed me in unimaginable ways.

"It's okay," he whispered, reading my mood. "We'll figure it out."

"Yeah. I know. But it's always going to be like this. Us stealing random minutes and, if we're lucky, hours during the day to be together."

"Hey. Look at me," he urged. His hand went under my chin, where he forced my head back until I had no choice but to give him my eyes. "We'll figure it out. I'll rob Father Time for the rest of my life if that's what it takes to get you. In the meantime, we've got phones." His whole face smiled. "Imagine how much fun we could have if you actually returned one of my texts."

My lips twitched. "You're awkward via text."

He smiled. "I'm awkward all the time, sweetheart." He paused to pointedly pluck my nipple. "It doesn't seem to have deterred you in the least."

And there it was again. A real, honest-to-God laugh bubbled in my throat, warming me in all the right places, but especially the one in my chest.

"Okay, Porter. We'll text and I won't let your awkwardness deter me."

"So generous," he deadpanned.

We lay there, our bodies flush, naked, and sated, for twenty minutes.

We talked. Nothing heavy. Just chitchat.

And we kissed, heavy, long, and wet.

And then Porter got up, got dressed, and got gone.

As he had promised after our first date, I spent the rest of the night touching my bruised and swollen lips, but they were split in a smile as I did it.

# TWENTY

## Porter

I'D BEEN OPTIMISTIC ABOUT HOW MUCH TIME I'D GET TO spend with Charlotte when we'd decided to grow something out of the intense connection we felt in the dark. I hadn't dated anyone since Catherine had died, but it couldn't be that hard to find time to date, right?

Wrong!

Charlotte and I had talked on the phone and texted *a lot*. But, in the two weeks since we'd officially started a relationship, we'd only managed to see each other four times. The grand total of those hours could have been counted on one hand. Two of those times had been when I'd stopped by her apartment on my way home from the restaurant. Not that her apartment was anywhere close to on my way home from the restaurant. But I'd been so desperate for more than a phone call that I'd taken the hour-long detour past her house. This had resulted in ten minutes of her smiling and a couple of kisses that weren't nearly deep enough to last me through the week. But it was so fucking worth it.

With both restaurants up and running, I barely had enough time for the kids. Forget about a social life. Thankfully, Charlotte understood. She was busy too. The other two of the four times we'd seen each other had been when she'd stopped in at the restaurant on her way home and watched me run around while she ate dinner alone at the bar.

I was starting to lose my mind. I craved that woman something fierce. And not just her body—though that was definitely part of it. But I missed seeing her face light with humor. And feeling her melt into my side as if she needed to be there to breathe. I missed the way her heart hammered in her chest each time I'd kiss her. And the way she moaned with contentment when I'd engulf her hand in mine.

But it was Charlotte, so if the phone and the text messages were all I could have of her, I'd still take it every single time.

It was now my first quasi-free night in over two weeks. Tanner was out of town, and I had a new manager working his first shift out of training. So, while I needed to physically be in the building in case he couldn't hack it, I didn't have to be actively working. I had a full four hours of mostly uninterrupted time to dedicate to a dinner and maybe some quiet time in my office with Charlotte. Yeah. Okay, fine. In the real world, it was a terrible excuse for a date night. And it sucked. Like, a lot. But it was the best we'd been able to swing in weeks.

We were silently sitting in our booth. Her eyes were aimed at the table while she used her thumb and her index finger to roll a torn-off edge of a cocktail napkin into a ball.

I knew what was coming, so I released her hand, leaned

back, and allowed her the time and space to draw up her courage.

She did this every day—whether in person or on the phone. One question about the kids. Never more. Never less. At first, it had been jarring, but then I'd figured that it was her way of easing them into her life. She'd caught me off guard more often than not on the phone. But, in person, I could always tell when the question was coming. She'd get quiet, emotionally pulling away from me even if she was physically in my arms. Her breathing would speed and she would nervously toy with the ends of her hair or a necklace or whatever she could get her hands on. After the first time, I'd learned to wait her out.

She'd ask.

I'd answer.

She'd swallow hard.

I'd kiss her and change the subject to something ridiculous.

She'd laugh.

And then we'd go back to doing whatever the hell we'd been doing or talking about before that one question had crossed her mind.

"How's Travis doing?" she finally asked.

I covered her hand, stilling her furiously circling fingers. "He's doing better. I talked to Dr. Whitehall this morning, actually. She's pleased with his progress. And I'm pleased that we haven't had to go back to the hospital in over a month."

"Good," she whispered before taking a sip of her wine.

I dipped my lips to her knuckles, murmuring, "You know, we could always have one of the waitresses deliver to the couch in my office?"

Her shoulders sagged, and I could feel the anxiety ebbing from her body.

I fucking hated the toll such a simple question took on her.

Especially a simple question about the two people I loved most in the world.

Her face remained unreadable, but her eyes flickered with humor. "And cost another innocent Porterhouse employee her job?"

I laughed. "Come on. I didn't fire anyone. No one has mentioned a word about overhearing us doing the deed. Besides, if they had, they've probably all spent the last two weeks building a class action sexual harassment case against me. At least let's make it worth my while if I'm gonna lose my ass in a lawsuit."

Her whole face lit as she smiled.

*Back to my Charlotte.*

I was so focused on her wide smile that I missed his approaching.

"Well, well, well. What do we have here?" Tanner drawled as he stopped at the end of our booth, sporting his signature I'm-about-to-screw-with-you-Porter shit-eating grin.

"What are you doing here?" I asked. "I thought you were out of town still?"

"I just got back. I swung by to pick up a bottle of champagne when Bethany told me you were back here with your *girlfriend*."

"And I'll remind you again, Tanner. Our bar does not double as your personal wine cellar. There's a liquor store two blocks over."

He ignored my comment and stared across from me. "You must be the infamous Charlotte Mills."

Her voice was even as she greeted, "And you must be Sloth."

Tanner twisted his lips in disbelief. "Sloth?"

Her face remained stoic and humorless in that way that I fucking adored as she said, "Yeah. Porter showed me a picture of you. I have to say, though, it must have been an old one, because you haven't aged well." She flipped her gaze to mine. "I was wrong before. You definitely got the looks in the family."

Tanner's jaw fell open in horror as I burst into laughter.

There was legitimately nothing sexier than watching Charlotte tap-dance on my brother's inflated ego.

Giving her hand a tight squeeze, I teased, "Is it too soon to be falling in love with you?"

"Yes. Entirely," she said dryly, but I knew my woman. And she was smiling on the inside.

I winked. "Okay. I'll wait until tomorrow."

A grin broke across her mouth, and Tanner blew out a hard breath, reminding us that he was still standing there.

"Oh, you were kidding," he laughed and slid into the booth on my side, forcing me to scoot over.

"Do you mind?" I complained.

"Not particularly," he replied. "So, Charlotte, do you have any idea how much my brother obsesses about you?"

"Seriously?" I grumbled.

She tipped her head to the side and slid her gaze to mine, her lips twitching almost imperceptibly. "You obsess about me?"

I shrugged. "No more than you obsess about me."

Her eyebrows shot up. "I wouldn't be so sure about that."

It was at that point that I suspected *she* was so focused on *my* smile that she missed the bright, white one approaching the table.

"She's lying. She's completely obsessed with you," Rita said, sliding into the booth beside her.

"Uhhh…" Charlotte drawled as she scooted over.

And then I quickly parroted her response when Tanner pushed up onto his elbows and leaned across the table, where Rita met him halfway for a quick peck on the lips.

Not even Charlotte's natural mask of mystery could contain her surprise.

"Hey, babe," Tanner said, reaching out to take Rita's hand in an uncomfortably familiar way I never realized we shared until that moment.

"Hey. Sorry I'm late. I lost my car keys," Rita replied, completely ignoring our palpable shock.

Tanner's face warmed. "You should have called. I still have your spare. I would have swung by and given it to you."

I literally could not form a single sentence as I flipped my gaze between the two of them, trying to make sense of the obvious.

Charlotte did not share this problem. "Are you two seeing each other?"

Rita's thick, black lashes batted innocently over her green eyes as she spoke out of the side of her mouth. "You aren't the only woman who landed a hot new man. We really need a wine night to catch up."

"I saw you an hour ago!" Charlotte exclaimed. "And literally every day this week. Why do we need a wine night for you to tell me you're dating Sloth?"

Tanner turned to me. "She's kidding about the Sloth thing, right? I seriously can't read her."

I backhanded his shoulder. "Please, God, tell me you are not sleeping with Rita! Her husband is Travis's doctor!"

Rita scoffed. "I am *not* married."

"Oh, that reminds me," Tanner said. "I talked to my attorney today. He received the signed divorce papers back from Greg."

I hit him again. "*Your* attorney is handling *her* divorce?"

Rita pursed her lips, stared dreamily at my womanizer brother, and clutched her imaginary pearls. "Thanks, honey. I really appreciate you taking care of that." She then said to Charlotte in a sugary-sweet tone that couldn't possibly be real—yet I somehow thought it was, "Do you guys mind if we do a little switch-a-roo on the seats so I can sit next to my guy?"

"Good idea," Tanner said as he climbed out of the booth, presumably to let me out.

But neither Charlotte nor I budged.

We just sat there.

Blinking.

Staring.

Waiting for the punch line.

What in the utter fuck was going on?

Rita plastered her front to Tanner's side.

He draped an arm around her and watched me expectantly. "You gonna get out of there or what?"

"Not until you tell—" The words died on my tongue when an idea struck me like a bolt of lightning. Sliding to my feet, I called, “Charlotte, can I have a word with you?”

She tore her accusing glare from Rita and asked, “Now?”

“Yes. In private.” I offered her a tight smile and flared my eyes in secret urgency.

She blinked but thankfully caught the hint and climbed out after me, leaving her purse on the bench.

“And bring your purse… I need…”—I glanced at Tanner as he sat down and pulled Rita down beside him—“ChapStick.”

“I don’t have any ChapStick,” she replied

“Oh, I do!” Rita exclaimed and then began digging through her bag.

Cupping Charlotte’s elbow, I moved close and chanted in a whisper, “Get your purse. Get your purse. *Get your purse.*”

Her back shot straight, but she followed my directions, mumbling, “You know what? I think I do have some.”

“We’ll be right back,” I told them, shuffling backward, bringing Charlotte with me.

“What are you doing?” she hissed as we hurried away.

“Give me your car keys.”

“What? Why? I thought you had to stay until closing.”

“Nope. *An owner* needs to be here until closing.” Peeking over my shoulder, I took one last glance to make sure Tanner wasn’t watching us before turning the corner toward the front door. “Sloth back there has his own set of keys to the restaurant, even if he does pretend that he doesn’t know how to use them.”

“We can’t leave now.” She threw on the brakes. “My best friend, who is on the rails after having her heart trampled on by one philandering man, just showed up with your famous brother, who I have to be honest, Porter, doesn’t look like Sloth at all. Like, not even a little bit, because I'm not completely convinced he's a human being and not a Greek god. I mean, you're sexy, Porter. But your brother—"

My mouth gaped open. "I'm standing right here!"

A slow smile curled her lips, and she winked. "I'm kidding. But seriously, he's going to chew her up and spit her out."

I cupped her face. "Probably. But all of that will still be the same tomorrow. If we can escape before Tanner realizes it, we can spend the next four hours doing whatever the hell we want. And, since we'll be at your apartment and not my restaurant, clothing is *not* required."

Her lips parted, and her eyes flashed dark. "Ohhhh."

"Yeah. 'Ohhhh.' But we have to go *now*. I don't have the energy to run a Ninja Warrior course against my brother to see which one of us is going to get laid tonight."

She laughed. But only for a second, because a blink later, she grabbed my hand and took off at a dead sprint through the dining room and out the front doors.

When we got to her car, I banged my knees on the steering wheel as I folded in, but it was a small price to pay to hear Charlotte's wild-child laugh as she jumped in on the other side.

"Go. Go. Go!" she yelled, pounding on the dashboard.

I peeled out of the parking spot, swiftly exiting the lot only to come to a screeching halt. A line of brake lights stretched out as far as I could see.

*Welcome to Atlanta traffic.*

"Well, that was anticlimactic," she deadpanned.

"Tell me about it." Going nowhere fast, I sighed and turned the radio on and skipped through the stations until the sound of AC/DC filled the small car.

No sooner than I moved my hand from the radio, she turned it off.

"Hey!" I objected.

Her face was carefully blank as she said, "You can drive. You can even program the position of your seat into one of the memory thingies. But you are *never* allowed to play AC/DC in my car. Her engine would seize, the transmission would fall out, and her wheels would shoot off, ruining the lives of hundreds of innocent bystanders and sending her into an early grave at the junkyard."

I held her stare. "Jesus. All that because of a little 'Highway to Hell'?"

She shrugged and looked back at the windshield. "Betty White takes her music seriously."

I bit my bottom lip, doing my best to stave a grin off. "Your car's name is Betty White?"

She looked back and didn't even crack a smile as she confirmed, "It was the obvious choice."

I laughed, loud and long.

So long that Charlotte finally gave the straight face up and burst out laughing as well.

"Get over here," I said, cupping the back of her neck and dragging her over the center console to plant a kiss on her sexy, sarcastic mouth.

Giggling, she pushed against my shoulder. "Porter, go. You're holding up traffic."

I kept her mouth against mine and blindly allowed the car to roll forward a few inches. "There. All caught up."

She continued to laugh, and I continued to drink it in.

God. I loved being with her. It didn't matter that we were sitting in standstill traffic, wasting precious minutes of the few hours we had alone. Toss my kids in the backseat and I'd have sat in that car with her for the rest of my life.

Releasing her, I righted myself in the driver's seat and tried to ignore the heavy weight settling in my chest.

Would I ever have that?

This free-spirited version of my broken woman, smiling and laughing with Travis and Hannah, who were as much a part of me as my heart and my lungs?

It had only been a few weeks. I was probably putting the cart before the horse. Even if she adored kids, I wouldn't have introduced them to her yet. Or, more accurately, her to them. It wasn't like I was divorced and dating again. My kids didn't have a mother. I could only imagine the hearts in Hannah's eyes if there was suddenly a woman in her life, doing all the things a mother should do with her daughter. The last thing I needed was them getting attached to a woman and then us falling apart.

Though, if the way my body hummed each time she aimed one of those secret smiles my way was any indication, I was getting pretty damn attached myself.

We hadn't gotten a full mile from the restaurant before my phone started ringing. I glanced down, fully expecting it to be Tanner ready to cuss me out for taking off.

But it wasn't, and my body jolted.

"Mom?" I answered before the phone had the chance to ring again. "Everything okay?"

"Hey, baby. Bad news."

My stomach dropped as Travis's face flashed through my

mind. “What’s wrong?”

“Relax. He’s fine,” she said, reading my anxiety.

I blew out a hard breath and shifted the phone to my other ear so I could anchor my hand on Charlotte’s thigh.

Her palm quickly covered my hand, her fingers tangling with mine.

“It’s Hannah, actually. She woke up with a fever earlier, so I gave her some Tylenol. But she’s coughing so badly she made herself throw up.”

“Shit,” I breathed, dropping my head back against the headrest.

“Don’t worry. I sent Travis to his room and disinfected everything she could have possibly touched in the last twenty-four hours. I’m sure it’s just a little bug, honey. But maybe she should come back to my house for a couple of nights.”

It should be noted that my mother was a saint.

“That sounds like a great idea.”

“Okay. I’ll get her bags packed. And I know you’re at work, but she asked if we could call you.”

Flashing my eyes to Charlotte, I found her studying me carefully.

And then I realized our biggest problem.

It was next to impossible to keep two such integral and important facets of my life separate at all times.

No matter how hard I tried, there would always be a crossover. Moments when the kids would be talking or fighting in the background while she and I were on the phone, forcing me to hurry into my room so she wouldn’t have to hear it. Or, now, while she sat silently at my side, my daughter wanting to talk to me because she didn’t feel well.

Those things were out of my control.

I didn't want to hurt Charlotte.

But, at the end of the day, I would always be a father who had to do what was best for his children.

"I'm sorry," I mouthed to her.

She tipped her head in question, her eyebrows knitting together.

I squeezed her thigh as I said into the phone, "Yeah. Put Hannah on."

Charlotte's body turned solid, and it fucking killed me, but I forged ahead when my baby girl's voice came through the line.

"I threw up."

Keeping my eyes on the car inching forward in front of me, I replied, "I heard. You feeling any better, sweet girl?"

"No," she groaned and then broke into tears. "Now, I can't have a Popsicle."

"What?" I laughed at the randomness of the statement.

"Grandma said I could have a Popsicle after dinner. But, when I threw up last time, you told me not to eat it because it would make my belly hurt."

I grinned. "But Grandma said you only threw up because you were coughing. So I don't think an ice pop is going to hurt anything. Tell Grandma I said you could have one." I paused before amending, "Just don't make it a red one on the off chance I'm wrong and you do throw it up."

"What about yellow?"

I chuckled. "Yeah. A yellow sounds perfect." *And easy to clean.*

She sniffled. "When are you coming home?"

I sighed and slid my gaze to Charlotte, who was chewing on her thumbnail like she had a personal vendetta against it, her eyes aimed out the window.

Fuck.

Fuck.

Fuck.

I was desperate for time with her.

But my baby needed me more.

"Soon," I whispered.

Her voice perked up. "Can I sleep in your bed until you get home?"

"Of course."

"Yay! Daddy said..." Her voice trailed off into the distance.

I rolled forward another few feet and put my blinker on so I could take the next turn back to the restaurant.

"Porter? You still there?" my mom asked.

"Yeah."

"Okay. I need to go before she beats down the door to get to Travis. But I'll see you when you get off tonight."

I stepped on the brakes as traffic once again became a standstill and closed my eyes. "Love you, Mom."

"Love you too," she replied, and then, just before she hung up, I heard her yell, "Hannah Ashley Reese, do not open that door!"

I put the phone in my lap and twisted to Charlotte. "I have to go home. Hannah's sick."

She didn't give me her eyes. "It's okay. I understand."

"Charlotte, I'm sorry about that."

Suddenly, she turned and her empty eyes leveled me.

"Don't do that," she whispered. "No apologies. Not in the darkness, but especially not in the light."

My eyebrows shot up. "We're in the light?"

She blinked, and tears sparkled in her eyes. "I'm wherever you are, Porter. And, for you, the darkness didn't even exist when you were on that phone."

"Sweetheart," I breathed, my heart breaking even as it swelled.

"I'm trying," she whispered.

I pulled her toward me and kissed her forehead. "I know you are."

"She's coughing?"

My hand spasmed, and I mumbled, "I'm sure it's just a cold."

Her fingers tensed at my arm, and then she shocked the hell out of me. "If you stop at the drug store, I'll help you pick out a good cough medicine and get you the proper dosage for her weight."

I blew out a hard breath as my stomach pitched. "You don't have to do that."

"Yeah. I do, Porter. I really, *really* do."

That was the exact moment I felt the seed plant in my chest.

My body roared to life, and an unbelievable calm washed over me.

It was warm and dense, a vast difference from the empty chill I usually carried. Eventually, it would overtake me and I'd be forced to recognize it. But, until then, I was going to lie back and let it grow.

We sat like that for several minutes.

Bumper-to-bumper traffic.
My lips to her forehead.
Her hand clinging to my arm.
But she was right.
We had done it in the light.

# TWENTY-ONE

## Charlotte

SUNLIGHT POURED IN THROUGH THE CURTAINS WHEN I was suddenly dragged out of sleep by a knock at my front door.

I was on my side, knees bent, hand tucked under my pillow, one leg over the covers, the other under, but even after I'd pried my eyes open, I was still very much in a dream world.

A hard, naked body was pressed against my back, one arm stretched out beneath my neck, the other wrapped around my ribs, his hand holding my breast, his heat enveloping me.

Porter had surprised me the night before by announcing that he'd not only taken the night off (to spend with me), but that he'd also asked his mom and dad to stay with his kids so we could have a whole twenty-four hours to ourselves. My heart had nearly leapt from my chest, and my body had *definitely* leapt into his arms. I couldn't remember the last time I'd been that excited about something.

We'd worn clothes for all of thirty minutes total that night. And that hadn't included drinking beers and eating Chinese food on my couch. (Begrudgingly, Porter had agreed to put pants on before opening the door for the delivery guy.)

I smiled and rolled against him, praying that whoever was at the door would disappear.

"What time is it?" he murmured without opening his eyes.

I lifted my head off his arm to look at the clock on the nightstand. "Eight fifteen."

"Mmmm," he purred sleepily. "Too early."

I pecked the tip of his nose. "See, this is what happens when you insist on the four-a.m. quickie."

His lids were still closed as he said, "Don't you dare try to blame me. You initiated that."

I grinned. I totally had. But I'd woken up much in the same way as I had moments earlier, only this time, it wasn't just Porter's hard body that was pressed up against me.

I kissed him again, this time on the lips—morning breath be damned.

He smiled and finally lifted his lids. "Morning."

"Morning," I breathed, running my hand over the top of his messy, blond hair.

"How'd you sleep?" he asked.

A pang of sadness hit my stomach.

*Better than I will tonight when you go home.*

"Good."

"Good. Then let's do it again," he said, nuzzling his head into the pillow before closing his eyes.

I chuckled and propped my head up with an elbow to the bed.

Porter was gorgeous, even at eight in the morning, with a thick layer of scruff covering his jaw and sleep—and sex—mussed hair. But it was the man inside that had captivated me so completely. The world was still spinning, but for the first time, I didn't feel the overwhelming need to keep up. Time moved slower when we were together.

Over the last few weeks, another of my fingers had slipped off the cliff, but my grip was still firm. Progress was progress though, no matter how small it was. I'd stopped going to the park and my old house. The urge was still there, but it almost felt liberating not to give in to it.

I'd known Porter for all of a month and I was leaps and bounds closer to reclaiming my life than I had been in ten years. And the most amazing part of all was that I was doing it by myself—with him at my side.

Porter lived by the rules. He never asked me questions, though I still told him answers. And, when I gave them to him, he didn't judge my truths. He had this incredible knack for recognizing the exact moment I'd escape into my head to distract myself from the pain of whatever had triggered me. And he'd patiently wait there for me to return. He never once gave me a reason to fake a smile. He'd just hold my hand and let me be. If I wanted to open up, I did. If I didn't, that was okay too. But I was never alone in the darkness. Not while he was there—even if that was only on the other end of a phone call.

But, right then, after having spent the night laughing, making love until the wee hours of the morning, and falling asleep wrapped in his arms, I felt something I had never experienced stir inside me.

And I didn't mean that I hadn't experienced it in the ten years since my world had fallen dark.

This particular *something* inside me was the likes I'd never felt in my *entire* life.

And it was the most beautiful something of all.

My nose stung as I pressed my lips together, fighting against the inevitable.

"Stop staring at me," he grumbled without opening his eyes.

I smiled, and it forced a single tear to slide down my cheek. I brushed it away and said, "It's just that you're really ugly in the mornings."

He chuckled and pulled me down so my head rested on his pillow. "That's not what you said at four a.m."

Closing my eyes, I tried to forget the reason I'd woken up in the first place, but there was another loud knock at the door.

Porter's eyes shot open. "You expecting company?"

"You're here. Rita is most likely shacked up with your brother. And my mom has a strict Saturday-morning-mimosa routine in which she doesn't leave the house until noon. So, no."

He twisted his lips. "You think it's one of the neighbors needing a bolster in morale?"

Exaggerating a groan, I rolled out of his arms and stood up. "Probably. Let me get my bra and panties on and see what I can do."

He laughed and sat up, his heated gaze following me as I ambled to my dresser, pulled out a T-shirt and sleep pants, and shrugged them on.

He grazed his teeth over his bottom lip. "Get rid of the clothes before you come back in here. My x-ray vision isn't what it used to be."

I smiled. "You used to have x-ray vision?"

He winked. "How else do you think I see you in the dark?"

"Wouldn't that be night vision?"

He stared off into the distance. "Well, what do you know? My superhuman abilities are multiplying."

My lips twitched as I rolled my eyes. "Okay, Captain America. While I get the door, why don't you try to unlock the powers that will enable you to put some pants on and start the coffee maker?"

"Captain America doesn't really have any powers besides his strength and a shield."

"Okay, then how about you use the shield to cover your ass while you get up and use your extra-strong finger to press the button on the coffee maker."

He barked a laugh at the same time I heard her voice.

"Charlotte?" she called from my living room. "Honey? It's Mom. I used my key, but just a heads-up, Tom's with me. So maybe put on some clothes before coming out."

"Shit," I breathed.

Porter's eyes got wide, and he scrambled from the bed, whispering, "What happened to mimosas?"

I shrugged and turned to the door. "No clue. But I'd highly suggest pants rather than the shield now."

Smiling, I listened to Porter's laughter fade behind the closed door as I headed down the hall. When I reached the living room, I found Tom and my mom standing in the entryway.

My lips fell as I took in my mom's ashen face, and Tom's arm anchored around her shoulders, his face equally pale.

Oh God.

Flashing my gaze between them, alarm bells screaming in my ears, I asked, "What's wrong?"

"Honey, we need to talk," she whispered, clutching her arms to her chest as if she were warding off a chill in the air. And, for the way the hairs on the back of my neck stood on end and goose bumps pebbled my skin, she might have been.

I looked at Tom, my voice thick as I asked, "What's going on?"

"Charlotte," he started, only to stop when his eyes flicked to something over my shoulder. "Shit. Sorry. I didn't realize you had company."

My mother slapped a hand over her chest, and her eyes filled with tears, but she wasn't looking at Porter. She was watching me, and her regret was palpable. "Oh God. He's the guy who made you so happy at the restaurant."

Porter's arm snaked around my hips from behind and I felt his lips in my hair, but not even his warmth against my back could drive away the frigid air swirling around the room.

"Hi. I'm Porter Reese. Nice to meet—"

I didn't let him finish. "Tom?" I prompted, taking a step forward.

Tom's eyebrows furrowed and he cut his gaze away uncomfortably.

My lungs began to burn, and my pulse spiked. There was only one reason I could think of to explain why Tom and my mom had shown up at my place at eight in the morning, looking like they'd seen a ghost.

And, suddenly, I was terrified they had.

Tom's gaze flicked back to minc, and his arm tensed around my mom. "We should talk in private, Charlotte."

I shook my head as my skin began to tingle. "Tell me."

Tom looked over my shoulder at Porter. "I'm gonna need you to leave, son."

I blinked, and then all of the oxygen was stolen from the room.

This was it. The truth that was going to set me free and then make me want to die.

My body became solid, but as my soul turned to liquid, I found myself drowning in everything I had once been.

Porter's front once again hit my back and his arms closed in around me, careful and insulating. But not even Porter's darkness could protect me from this.

"Not happening," Porter replied gruffly.

"Tell me," I choked.

"Honey..." my mother started, pausing long enough to collect herself before continuing. "This is a private—"

"Tell me!" I yelled. What started as a chin quiver quickly worked its way down to a full-body shake as adrenaline ravaged my system.

My mother jumped and Tom instinctively took a step toward me, but it was Porter who kept me on my feet.

"Breathe," he urged into the top of my hair as he attempted to tuck me into his side, but I was having none of it.

I didn't want comfort. I wanted the answers, but I was afraid I wanted different answers than they were going to give me.

Pushing out of Porter's arms, I stood on my own two

shaking legs just like I had the day my boy had been taken and looked Tom directly in the eye. "Please."

He sucked in a sharp breath, straightened his back, and then gave me the *words* I was so desperate to hear. "The body of a baby was uncovered at a construction site they were breaking ground on late last night."

My chest caved in, and a wave of nausea rolled in my stomach.

There it was.

The moment I'd been waiting so long for.

The *words* I'd prayed so many times I'd never hear. And then, years later, the ones that I prayed would finally allow me to let go.

"Is it him?" I asked without actually feeling anything.

Porter got close again, hovering without touching me.

My mom reached out, tears pouring from her eyes.

Tom's face contorted as if I'd asked him to shoot me.

And I stood there, pleading for someone to finally end my nightmare.

"We don't have a cause of death or positive ID yet, but—" Out of his back pocket, Tom produced a photo and lifted it my way.

I slapped a hand over my mouth, and the ground rumbled beneath my feet. The past roared to life even as I clung to the present. I would have recognized that pacifier clip anywhere. It had been last seen clipped to the front of my son's shirt. I'd had it custom made for him before I'd even known he was a boy. Call it mother's intuition or whatever, but I'd felt it in my bones.

He had been my son.

And, now, he was gone.

A dark, guilt-ridden part of my soul died as I stared at the picture of that blue-and-white-polka-dot ribbon, the pacifier he had once suckled still connected to the end, five letters monogrammed in thick block font to form what I now knew was the most painful *word* in the English language.

Lucas.

And then, suddenly, even though I'd had ten years of warning, the world finally stopped.

# TWENTY-TWO

## Porter

I HAD NO IDEA WHAT WAS IN THAT PICTURE, BUT IT WASN'T hard to follow the bouncing ball, though it was impossible to grasp the reality of it all.

Her son was dead. They'd found his body, which had been buried for God only knew how long while she'd spent ten years living and breathing but buried right alongside him.

He wasn't even my child and the pain was damn near crippling. I couldn't imagine the hurricane blowing inside her.

When she stumbled on weak legs, colliding with my chest, I couldn't gather her in my arms fast enough. Turning her, I supported her weight. Her back arched as she curved her front against mine. Her heart raced and her chest heaved as the unfathomable devoured her. And, through it all, I did the only thing I could. I held her tight, waiting for her to explode and cursing the moment when her guttural cries would tear through the room like a tornado of devastation, leveling us all.

I would have given anything to carry her back to the bedroom. To hit rewind and go back to when she had been peacefully sleeping at my side. Her breathing even. Her heart slow. Her body languid. Her mind still. The scars on her soul temporarily forgotten.

The truth was I could hold her until my arms fell off, but I couldn't make this better for her. Part of her had been missing long before I'd met her, but the grieving process was just getting started, and there was absolutely nothing I could do to soften that blow.

But that didn't mean I wasn't going to try.

She didn't scream.

She didn't cry.

She didn't wail or shake her fist at the heavens.

She didn't even move.

"I'm here," I mumbled into the top of her hair, repeatedly kissing the side of her face. "I'll stop with you. It's just me and you, Charlotte."

She didn't respond. Honestly, I wasn't even sure she was breathing anymore.

She was still.

Utterly. Completely. Eerily so.

"Honey." Her mom appeared beside us.

My muscles tensed as my body screamed in objection, but when Charlotte pivoted in her direction, I let her go.

Charlotte didn't move into her mother's open arms.

Stepping away from us both, she stated, "I need coffee." And then, robotically, she tilted her head back to catch my gaze. "You want some?"

Calm. Cool. Collected.

Not a tear in sight. Steady hands. Square shoulders.

Fuck. Fuck. Fuck.

It wasn't just her face anymore. Her whole aura was blank. Not even I could find the emotion hidden within.

It was worse than the cries I'd expected because it was the first time since I'd met Charlotte that I realized there wasn't even enough of her left to explode.

"Charlotte," I rasped. "Come back, sweetheart."

But I didn't mean physically. She was gone, and it scared the hell out of me.

Reaching out to catch her hand, I tangled our fingers together, desperately trying to get a read on her. She didn't grip it tight with anxiety. Nor did she give it a sweet squeeze. But, worst of all, she didn't even pull it away in an attempt to hide.

She just held it, limp and loose.

Physically there but mentally and emotionally a million miles away.

I moved closer, worry ricocheting inside me, and whispered, "Let's go sit in the darkness."

She offered me a reassuring smile so fake that it appeared as though it were made of plastic. "Let's stay in the light today, Porter."

I searched her face. "I don't know where you are right now, but I promise you this isn't the light. Let me in. I'll come with you, wherever you want to go. I'm there."

After pulling her hand from mine, she rested her palms on my chest. Then, keeping her gaze down, she absently traced the seam at the neck of my T-shirt. "I've been waiting a long time to know where my baby was. Now, I know. This is as close to the light as I'm ever going to get."

The breath rushing from my lungs felt as though I'd been hit with a sledgehammer.

She had a point. A sad, depressing, tragic point. But a point nonetheless.

I held her empty gaze, searching for a glimmer of the woman I'd been falling in love with over the last month, but if she was in there, I couldn't be sure.

Unfortunately, she didn't give me long to look. Spinning, she briskly headed for the kitchen.

"Charlotte, let me get the coffee," her mom said, following after her.

I stood frozen, unable to move.

Everyone reacted different to tragedy. I knew this first-hand. Hell, I'd fought a pond one time.

But this was different, and I had no fucking idea what to do.

Did I give her space?

Did I follow her and insist she talk to me?

Did I carry her to the bedroom, close the blinds, and force her into the darkness confessional with me?

If I stuck with the rules, my only option was to wait for her to come to me, but that felt like the impossible.

But, if I broke them, I risked breaking her too.

I watched her over the bar as she plundered around her small kitchen. Her mother frantically tried to stop her, but Charlotte ignored her pleas and went about gathering coffee, retrieving mugs from the cabinet, filling the carafe with water, and then pouring it into the machine. Her face was emotionless, and her movements were smooth, not at all jerky or rough with distress. She was on autopilot.

When she'd finished filling two mugs to the brim, she hand-delivered one to me in the exact same spot she'd left me, but this time, she was standing an arm's length away.

I took the coffee but kept my gaze trained on hers and said the only thing I could think of. "Let me in."

She kept her eyes aimed at her cup as she swirled the creamy, brown liquid inside, muttering, "Trust me. You don't want in on this one."

I painfully closed my eyes and shook my head. When I opened them, I glanced over at Tom, who was standing a few feet away, watching her, his eyes narrow and assessing.

"Charlotte," he called. "I'm gonna wait for more information before going to talk to Brady. He's gonna want answers that I don't have right now. You want to go with me when I do that?"

She looked up at me, but her words were for Tom. "I don't think that would be a good idea." Then her words were for me, and they formed the most ridiculous statement I had ever heard. "You should probably go."

"No," I answered firmly. Inching forward, I switched my coffee to my left hand and curled my right around the back of her neck. Then, bending at the knees, I lowered myself into her line of sight. "If you *want* me to leave, sweetheart, that's one thing. I won't like it. And it will fucking kill me. But, if that's what you *need*, I'm gone. However, short of you kicking me out, I'm not going anywhere. I told you: I'd stop with you." I gave her neck a squeeze. "*Always*, Charlotte."

A wave rocked through her empty eyes, revealing the tiniest flicker of my Charlotte hiding within. Relief blasted through me.

"You want to stop?" I asked. "Pretend this isn't happening right now?"

Her chin quivered as she nodded, her eyes filling with tears.

Using her neck, I guided her against my front, her body plastering to mine. Coffee sloshed to the floor as she looped her arms around my hips. Not even then did she cry, but she held me so tight that I thought she was trying to meld our bodies into one. Which, I had to admit, I wouldn't have minded.

"Then we'll stop," I whispered before kissing the top of her head.

Her mom rushed over, taking both of our mugs. Tears streamed from her chin as she watched her daughter tightening her hold on me and her fists clutching the back of my shirt. She kissed the back of Charlotte's head, and then looked up at me.

"I'm going to stay, but I'll keep out of your way."

I nodded.

Tom walked over and rubbed Charlotte's back before giving her shoulder a squeeze. "I need to get back to work, babe. I'll check in later."

When Charlotte didn't reply or acknowledge him, he dipped his chin at me, pressed a kiss to Charlotte's mom's temple, and headed for the door.

And then we were alone.

Well, almost. Charlotte's mom, whose name I would later learn was Susan, got busy cleaning the already spotless apartment. Charlotte was a minimalist. There were only so many times you could rearrange the two knickknacks on the bar or dust the four framed pictures on the wall. But, true to her word, Susan stayed out of our way.

And, true to my word, I pretended that nothing had happened that morning.

Seriously, for the way my chest ached and my mind swirled, it was an Oscar-worthy performance.

Charlotte and I sat on the couch, my feet propped on her coffee table, her legs angled over mine. She didn't own a TV, but I grabbed her laptop and put on some mind-numbing comedy I'd found on Netflix. Neither of us watched it.

Her dark browns stared off into the distance, lost in thoughts, and my blues stared at her, lost in worry.

She absently played with my fingers, weaving them together before letting go, only to start the process over again, while I lazily drew circles on her legs.

We talked occasionally, but about nothing.

She even half laughed once when I made a joke about the train wreck that was Rita and Tanner.

As the minutes turned into hours, Susan offered to make breakfast. Charlotte declined, but she accepted coffee, which she held against her chest, untouched, until it got cold. Then she discarded it.

Lunch went much the same way, only this time, she balanced a plate with a sandwich in her lap until I finally took it from her and set it on the table.

Together, we sat on that couch all day, curled up, holding each other, lost somewhere on the infinite horizon between darkness and light, delaying the inevitable.

Shortly after five in the afternoon, Charlotte drifted off to sleep and I snuck out from under her long enough to call my mom to check in on the kids and let her know I was going to be late—*really late*. She readily offered to stay another night, but I knew she needed to get home. She and my dad were heading out of town for their annual two-week-long anniversary trip to Maine in the morning. I'd felt guilty as hell when I'd asked her to stay the first night with the kids, but with the prospect of having no babysitter for a full fourteen days, my desperate need for time with Charlotte won out. And because my mom was, well…a saint, she'd agree before I'd fully finished asking the question. But I couldn't ask her to make that sacrifice again.

As I watched Charlotte sleeping peacefully on the couch, knowing that a superstorm was brewing inside her but also knowing that my kids needed me at home, I once again found myself trapped between the two facets of my life.

And, suddenly, I was in that sinking car all over again, being forced to choose between two people I loved and knowing I was going to fail one of them.

Closing my eyes, I sucked in a sharp breath and tucked my phone into my back pocket.

The truth was, Charlotte wasn't the only one on that couch pretending. I'd been doing it for years. Hell, I even pretended not to pretend when I knew I was pretending.

If I expected her to face reality, I had to do the same.

It was going to hurt. No. It was going to kill.

But maybe opening myself up, feeling it, and embracing the pain was the only way to truly let it go.

Numb wasn't working anymore. Not for me. And definitely not for Charlotte.

It was time for it to end.

After walking over to the couch, I settled on the edge, a

newfound resolve flooding my veins while dread pooled in my gut. "Wake up, sweetheart," I whispered, brushing her hair out of her face.

Her sleepy lids flipped open, and for the briefest of seconds, they held actual warmth, her lips curling up at the sides as she unfurled from her ball and wrapped herself around me. And then, with one single blink, her face went blank. "Are you leaving?"

I smiled weakly. "I need you to go somewhere with me."

Her eyebrows pinched together, wrinkling her forehead. "Where?"

I bent low and touched my lips to hers. "Somewhere. You up for it?"

She searched my face as she sat up, concern etched in her features. "If you *need* me to go with you, then, yeah, Porter, I'm up for it."

I kissed her again, deeper and filled with apology.

"It's gonna suck," I mumbled against her lips.

She didn't miss a beat before murmuring, "Hanging out with you usually does."

Heartbroken. Grieving. Shattered. And still making jokes at my expense.

*Charlotte.*

*My Charlotte.*

I laughed. Loudly. Far more loudly than anyone should have laughed on that day. But that was exactly how I knew we were both going to be okay.

After whispered goodbyes and brief hugs, we left Susan at Charlotte's apartment.

It was obvious she wasn't thrilled that we were leaving,

but it was also clear she liked the way Charlotte tucked herself under my arms and nuzzled in close when she was ready to go.

"We'll be back in a little while," I assured.

Susan nodded and took Charlotte's face in her hands. "You need anything, you call me, okay? I'm going to be right here waiting for you."

"Thanks, Mom," Charlotte whispered.

"Of course, baby." Susan stepped away, her face blazing with a myriad of emotion, making it clear that her daughter did *not* get her ability to hide in plain sight from her mother.

Then, with my arm draped around her shoulders, her arm hooked around my hips, and her other hand resting on my stomach, we left her apartment as two shattered people for what I hoped would be the very last time.

# TWENTY-THREE

## Tom

Tom Stafford's gut was sour as he sat behind his desk at the police station. That was the one notification he'd never wanted to make. Those were his girls. Well, Susan was more than that—she was the one woman he had every intention of keeping until he was six feet deep. That relationship had been a slow burn, grown over time. He'd been in love with that woman long before he'd even asked her on their first date.

But Charlotte was different. She was part of him. The daughter he'd never gotten to watch grow up. He hated the hand life had dealt her, but no matter what, Charlotte would *always* be his girl. They had a rock-solid bond forged through heartache and memories. Nothing could break that.

The case of Lucas's disappearance had been cold since day one, but that didn't mean Tom had stopped trying to locate that little boy. Dead end after dead end, he forged ahead, refusing to stop until he'd found him. There hadn't been a day in the almost ten years when he hadn't cracked that tattered case file open and tried desperately to read between the lines for any clue to the whereabouts of Lucas Boyd.

But each day reaped the same bounty: None.

The construction site where Lucas's body had been found was only two miles from the park where he'd gone missing. The police, the FBI, and hundreds of volunteers had scoured every inch of those woods at least a dozen times over the first few days after he'd been taken. Hell, Tom had personally combed that grid at least five of those times. But, judging by the coroner's initial assessment and the estimated age of the remains, Lucas Boyd had been in that shallow grave since day one.

Guilt settled heavily in his chest. He could have ended that nightmare for Charlotte almost a decade earlier. Only he hadn't. And it fucking corroded his soul, knowing that.

Rocking back in his chair, he sipped off the lip of a paper cup filled with coffee so strong that he probably should have chewed it. He'd gotten the call around eleven the previous night that the badly deteriorated remains of a baby had been discovered, and he had been at the station by eleven twenty. The moment he saw the filthy baby-blue-striped onesie Lucas had last been seen wearing, his stomach had dropped.

But there were a lot of little blue-striped onesies floating around the world. It was that damn pacifier clip with the boy's name stitched into the side that had lit Tom on fire. Fuck. For as long as he'd been searching, right then, he hated with a vengeance that it had been found. Or, more accurately, that it had ever needed to be found in the first place.

He hadn't slept a wink in the hours that had followed. He hadn't even gone home. Instead, he'd decided to break protocol and put his girls out of their misery once and for all. He drove straight to Susan's house, sat in his car, waited for the day to break, and prepared to crush the heart of the woman he loved. Then he was going to be forced to ask that same woman to help him deliver the news that was going to shatter her daughter.

The only comfort he could find was knowing that he could finally give both Susan and Charlotte the closure they so desperately deserved. Though it didn't feel anything like relief as he watched Susan fall to her knees. And definitely not when he watched Charlotte slip so deeply behind her walls that he feared she would never reemerge. But, ultimately, that closure was the only consolation he was ever going to get—unless he could find the person responsible.

Lucas was gone and there was nothing he could do to change that. But his case was far from closed.

A newfound hope had exploded within him from knowing there had to have been some kind of evidence on the body. Forensics had come a long way since he'd first joined the force over thirty years earlier. He had faith that the lab would find him something to go on. And it was that same faith that had him sitting at the station, staring at his computer screen, furiously refreshing his email in hopes the report would appear.

He'd been texting Susan all afternoon, and from what she was saying, Charlotte was still very much in denial. The silver lining being that it seemed she had finally found a man who could handle her with the care she deserved. Charlotte hadn't shared with Tom or her mother that she and Porter had rekindled whatever connection they'd witnessed that night at The Porterhouse. But, from seeing the way she clung to him as if he could magically solve the world of hurt Tom had dropped at her feet, it was clear they had definitely rekindled something serious.

"Hey, Tom!" Charlie Boucher, his longtime partner, called in a thick New York accent, a stark contrast to the good ol' Southern boys who made up over ninety percent of the department.

Tom turned and found him striding toward him from across the room, a manila envelope in his hand lifted in the air.

Shooting to his feet, Tom lurched toward him. "That my results?"

Charlie shrugged. "Picked 'em up at the lab. We got good news and bad. And, because the world is a seriously fucked-up place, they're both the same thing."

Tom snatched the envelope and tore into it, blood thundering in his ears.

Charlie dropped his ass into the chair next to Tom's desk, kicked his feet out in front of him, and announced, "It's not Lucas Boyd."

# TWENTY-FOUR

## Charlotte

"WHERE ARE WE GOING?" I ASKED PORTER AS HE DROVE my car down the quiet roads on the outskirts of the city.

He had the windows down, the radio off, and his hand latched onto my thigh. The warm April air whipped through the car, but I was too numb to feel it.

If I didn't specifically think about the fact that Lucas was gone, it was really no different than any other day. He'd been gone for years. It wasn't as if someone had snatched him from my arms that morning. Or so I'd convinced myself as the gut-wrenching pain of Tom's announcement had buckled my knees.

I'd shut down, and it had been a conscious decision. Just as it had been the first week after Lucas had gone missing when I went back to school. I wasn't built to handle that kind of emotional upheaval.

The emptiness was easier.

And that's saying something because the emptiness was agonizing.

"We're here," Porter replied in a grim tone.

"Uh…" I glanced around at the road as he pulled onto the shoulder. And then my heart stopped when he put my car in park at the foot of a small concrete bridge that looked a lot like an overpass, but instead of a highway, it straddled the Chattahoochee River.

"This is where it started," he said stiffly as his hand clamped down on my leg surprisingly tight, his face etched with panic. He lifted a finger and pointed out the windshield. "I watched her drive through that guardrail, not even so much as a brake light as warning."

"Oh God," I gasped, covering his hand with mine.

A few cars zipped past us from opposite directions, the sounds of their engines unable to drown out the tremendous ache in his whispers as he confessed, "I've never come back. In the three years she's been gone, I've never come back here."

"Of course not," I breathed, squeezing his hand tight. "Why would you?"

His blue gaze cut to me. "Because this is where it started." He pulled his hand away and opened his door, pushing it wide before finishing with, "And this is where it needs to end."

I'd been wrong before. *That* was when my heart stopped.

"Porter!" I yelled, scrambling out after him, fear icing my veins. I watched in horror as he climbed the guardrail and then started down the embankment. "Porter, stop!" I screamed, slinging my leg over the hot metal, bile creeping up my throat.

And praise God, he actually listened.

Turning to face me, he looked at me like I was crazy. “What?”

“What?” I screamed back at him, incredulous, the first tears of the day hitting the backs of my eyes. “What the fuck are you doing?”

“Going for a swim,” he answered—again, like *I* was the crazy person.

Blinking, I gave myself a minute to consider the possibility that I really was the crazy person, because absolutely nothing was making sense. After I took inventory of the situation and decided I was *not*, in fact, having a nervous breakdown, I asked, “Are you having a nervous breakdown?”

“Not that I'm aware of,” he replied evenly. So evenly that I figured it meant he absolutely *was* having a nervous breakdown.

I got my feet back on the ground on his side of the guardrail and curled a finger in his direction. “Porter, baby,” I said softly. “Come here. You're not going for a swim. That water is gross and there are probably alligators or, at the very least, snakes,” I guessed.

He cocked his head to the side but thankfully took several steps toward me. “I know it's gross, Charlotte. I've been living with that filth on me for the last three years. I'm ready to get rid of it.”

“You can't—”

“I can,” he stated definitively. “I'm so fucking sick and tired of living with this shit. I hate her for killing herself and trying to take my kids with her. But that's on her. I can't change that. The only thing I can change is how I feel about what happened. I've spent a lot of years feeling guilty for failing her.”

My breath caught, and my throat started to burn. God, did I know that feeling.

It was the one wound that would never heal.

"Porter, you didn't fail her."

His lips thinned, and he nodded sadly. "I did. I really did. I should have seen it coming. I knew she'd been struggling, but I didn't realize it had gotten that bad. We'd been dealing with Travis's health issues for as long as I could remember, and she was always so fucking optimistic about everything, but the day they finally told us he was going to need a heart transplant, she couldn't handle it."

I'd lied. Twice. *That* was the moment my heart stopped.

Oh. My. God.

"What?" I croaked, throwing a hand up to cover my mouth as I stumbled back a step, the guardrail breaking my fall.

"Shit. I'm sorry, I shouldn't have brought up the kids."

I shook my head. That wasn't at all why I was upset. "Your son had a heart transplant?" I choked out behind my hand.

He twisted his lips. "Well, not yet."

"Why not!" I yelled, my chest aching at yet another tragedy Porter and I had in common.

His eyes narrowed. "He's only been on the list for about six weeks. It's why I've been so frantic to keep him well over the last few months. If he's sick when that call comes in with a donor, we're screwed."

"Oh God. His pulmonary issues are because of his heart?"

"Shit," Porter muttered, and then he pulled me into his arms. "Christ, Charlotte. It's okay. He's okay. He's been doing better thanks to Dr. Whitehall. She even had the head of pediatric cardiology at TCH do a phone consult with our cardiologist last week."

My chest felt like it was being squeezed in a vise. God, Porter had truly lived through hell. I still remembered that day at the doctor's office when Lucas had been diagnosed. It had been the most painful moment of my life—at that point anyway.

I clung to his shoulders as if I could transfer my sympathies through body heat alone. "I'm so sorry. I didn't know. I—"

Using my arms, he shifted me away from his so he could see my face. "Sweetheart. He's *okay*. My boy's a fighter. He'll get through this."

"But what if—" I started, but that's as far as I got.

"No. Don't even think about it. I spend a lot of time in the darkness, but Travis's health is not allowed there. He's going to be fine. He's going to get that transplant and live to be an old man. That is the only option. Therefore, it will be the only result. You got me?"

Just like with Lucas, I knew too much to believe that. But, if Porter wanted to pretend, I wouldn't be the one to ruin that for him.

I nodded. "You're right. He's going to be fine."

"Good. Now, we have other things to talk about," Porter said, tucking hair behind my ear.

"What?" I whispered.

He swept his thumbs under my eyes. "You're crying."

I sniffled. "Crap. Sorry. This is your nervous breakdown, not mine."

He grinned and repeated, "My nervous breakdown?"

I swung my hand out to the side. "We're at *the* bridge. You're going for a swim in the gross water. You think you've been dirty for three years."

He chuckled and dipped his lips to my forehead. "I can pause my nervous breakdown. It's been a terrible day and you haven't cried at all, and then you find out my kid needs a new ticker and you burst into tears. Anything you want to talk about?" He paused. "Besides the obvious."

I cut my gaze off to the side in time to see another car had breezed past us. "Besides the obvious? Nope."

"Right," he whispered. "We still pretending?"

I gave him my eyes back as they welled with tears all over again. Shit. "I—uh…"

He kissed my nose and didn't make me finish. "Okay, then. Let's get back to my nervous breakdown."

I swallowed hard. "Wait. You aren't really having a nervous breakdown, are you?"

His shoulders shook as he chuckled. "No."

"Okay. Then yes, let's get back to that."

Leaning forward, he whispered, "I'm ready to let go. That guilt has been devouring me for too long. I did the best I could that day, Charlotte. Was it perfect? Fuck no. But I can't change it. The old Porter Reese is somewhere at the bottom of that river. I'm ready to get him back."

Motion at the ground drew my attention to his feet. He was stepping out of his shoes.

"I'm not sure you have to swim in the—Porter!" I yelled as he suddenly took off running down the rocky embankment.

He didn't dive in, but he didn't slow as he waded into the

murky water. And then, all at once, he disappeared under the surface.

"Shit," I muttered, toeing my shoes off just in case I had to rush in on a rescue mission, all the while scanning the area for alligators.

Less than a second later, his head reemerged, his voice echoing as he boomed, "Holy fuck, this is cold!" But he was smiling. Huge and completely unlike anything I'd ever seen him wear before, and that was odd because, when we were together, Porter smiled a lot—we both did.

But this smile, it was beautiful. It actually hurt to look at because it was so fucking genuine that it made me jealous. I didn't have a nasty river to dive into in order to symbolically reclaim my life.

All I had was a son who was missing…

"Oh God," I breathed. My mouth began to water as my stomach rolled.

My knees shook, and I literally could not force my lungs to fill with air.

I was bone dry and drowning on the banks of a river.

It was a somewhat out-of-body experience as I watched him climbing back up that embankment, his jeans leaving a trail of water across the dry rocks and dirt, his shirt clinging to his strong arms and his chest. His smile never faltering until he stopped in front of me.

Extending his hand, he said, "Hi. I'm Porter Reese."

And that was when I fell, a strangled cry escaping my mouth. "He's dead."

# TWENTY-FIVE

## Porter

THE SOUND OF HER CRY TORE THROUGH ME, SLAYING ME AS my mind struggled to process her words. I dove forward, catching her before her knees hit the ground.

"He's dead. My baby's gone," she sobbed, reality slashing her with every syllable.

Water poured from my sopping-wet clothing as I held her tight against my chest, wishing I could do more.

Clearly, Charlotte was done pretending.

"I know," I whispered, pressing my lips to her temple.

"This was supposed to be easier," she cried, her hand shoving at my shoulder. "This was what I wanted. It's not supposed to hurt like this."

"I know, sweetheart." I kissed her again, staring without seeing over her head as cars rushed by. The world still moved even as I desperately tried to stop it for her.

Her body bucked with sobs. "It's been ten years, Porter.

It shouldn't hurt this badly. I should be relieved. I should be grateful that he hasn't been suffering for all these years. I should…"

And that was when I broke every rule we had ever created.

The rules weren't helping her.

They weren't helping me.

They weren't helping *us*.

The darkness was still the loneliest place on Earth, no matter how much company you had. Charlotte and I had been kidding ourselves. We didn't share the darkness.

Together, we lived in the blinding light of day. It was an ugly, desolate place where horrible things happened to good people.

But love grew there.

I had known that first moment I'd seen Charlotte Mills.

And there was nothing in the world I wouldn't do to hold on to that.

Even if that meant facing the jagged blade of reality.

I unwrapped my arms and grabbed her shoulders, giving her a gentle shake just to be sure I had her attention. "Stop saying how you *should* feel. There is no right way to feel when you find out your child is gone. I don't care if it's been ten seconds or ten years. You are allowed to feel. You're allowed to hurt. Hell, Charlotte, maybe that's the key. Pretending won't change anything. The truth will always be waiting for you. You've got to let it hurt, sweetheart. Let that pain in. Let it light you on fire. Let it take you to your knees. Let the avalanche overtake you. Let it break every bone in your body until you think nothing is left." I paused and lowered my voice. "And then let it go."

"He was my son. I can't let him go."

"No. You are absolutely right. But you *can* let go of the guilt from that day. Look, I can't stand here and tell you that you have nothing to feel guilty about any more than I can look in the mirror and tell myself that same thing. But I *can* tell you that you have to let that shit go. It's killing you, Charlotte. It's going to be the most painful thing you have ever experienced. But you *can* let it go. And you have to. Because that is the only way you can move on."

"I don't want to move on!" she screamed, her whole body tense.

I made my voice soft and tipped my head down to rest my forehead on hers. "Yes, you do. I see it in your eyes every time you look at me. Every time you laugh at my stupid jokes. Every time you ask me that one single, solitary question about my kids. But just because I have a fucked-up past too does not mean I'm your ticket out of hell. You have to find that within yourself."

She laughed without humor and stepped out of my reach, tears pouring down her face. "There is no ticket out of this kind of hell, Porter. And if you think that little dip in the river was anything more than you pretending to have found yours, then you're worse off than I am."

I blew out a hard breath and hated myself before I ever said the words. But she was about to go back into hiding, and this time, I feared she wouldn't be coming back.

"He's dead, Charlotte."

She blanched, staring at me with feral eyes.

"I know you love him. And I know there is nothing you wouldn't give up to have him back. But there is nothing you can do anymore. He will *always* be your son. Ten million years from now, that will still be true. But the opposite of love isn't hate the way I always thought. It's agony, sweetheart. And you've been living with that for too long. Let. It. Go."

She blinked again, and then her whole face crumbled. "He's my *son*."

"And he loved you. Do you think—" I didn't make it any further because her body turned to stone.

"What?" she breathed.

My eyebrows knitted together. "What, what?"

"He was a baby, Porter. He didn't love me. He *needed* me. And I failed him."

My chest got tight. Fucking hell. She didn't know that her son loved her. I'd never forget the day Travis first told me that he loved me. Of course, I'd already fallen crazy in love with him. He was five and Catherine and I had been married for just over a year, but knowing he loved me had ignited something I hadn't known existed inside me. Kids did that to you. They made you whole even when nothing was missing.

From that point on, Travis would always be my son. Maybe not by blood, but he was mine all the same. Love had bound us together. I'd asked Catherine that very same night if she would allow me to legally adopt him, and I'd never looked back.

And it cut me deep, knowing Charlotte never got that from her child.

"Oh, Charlotte." I closed the distance between us and pulled her into a hug. Her arms remained slack at her sides, but I didn't let it deter me. "Of course he loved you. You were his mom."

Her breath hitched, and she stammered, "And…I failed him."

"And he *still* loved you," I whispered.

"He shouldn't. I left him alone."

"And he *still* loved you."

Her legs wobbled and she circled her arms around my hips. "I chose to help a complete stranger over taking care of my own son."

"And he *still* loved you."

"Why?" she whined.

"Because, just like he will always be your son, ten million years from now, you will *still* be his mom. Nothing you did changes that."

And then Charlotte Mills finally let it go.

Her knees gave out and the weight of ten years' worth of guilt swallowed her.

She cried, mumbling unintelligible words. Some I assumed were apologies to her son. Some were apologies to me. Some were angry and aimed at the universe. Some were bitter and aimed at herself.

All of them wrecking her.

But, in some way, all of them healing her as well.

This wasn't the end for Charlotte. It was very much the beginning.

And, no matter the cost, I was going to be there every step of the way.

After about fifteen minutes of standing, Charlotte sank to the ground. I followed her down and pulled her into my side, where she continued to cry for what seemed like an eternity.

I helplessly held her while unconditional love and guilt

destroyed her.

And, during that time, I stared down at that river and let it all destroy me too.

We sat there for well over an hour. Holding each other. Grieving pasts we couldn't change.

The same pasts that had brought us together.

And, ultimately, the same pasts that would tear us apart.

# TWENTY-SIX

## Tom

"NO FUCKING WAY," TOM STAFFORD GROWLED, HIS HAND shaking as he stared at the DNA results for the unidentified baby Johnny Doe. "This has to be some sort of mistake."

Charlie Boucher uncomfortably rocked onto his toes. "No mistaking it. Now, before you lose your shit, I did discover a few things that I think you might find interesting."

Tom jerked his head up and scowled.

"Right. Okay," Charlie mumbled. "They got three different DNAs off the body. The first from the clothing. Definitely Lucas Boyd. The second from the body. Definitely *not* Lucas Boyd. And one from the lining of the bag he was discovered in. A woman. And this did *not* belong to Charlotte Mills. We got no hits in the database on it. However, the first bit I found interesting is it appears that the unidentified child is related to the unidentified woman. As in…she was his mother."

Tom blinked, the wheels in his head starting to turn. "Cause of death?"

"It's an old body, Tom," he warned.

"We've done more with older," Tom shot back.

Charlie shook his head. "There's no clear cause as of yet—at least, not physically. They sent a few samples off, but it's going to take a while to get the pathology and toxicology back."

Fuck. He knew from experience that that shit could take forever.

Tom pinched the bridge of his nose and dropped the file on his desk. His sour gut turned downright toxic as he tried to figure out how the hell he was going to explain all of this to Charlotte. Break her heart all over again. Fuck. Why the hell had he told her before he had been positive?

Oh, right. Because he'd been so damn hopeful that it was finally over for all of them.

Himself included.

Tom knew he was a good cop. But he was too close to this investigation. He should have passed it off years earlier, when he and Charlotte had started getting close, but he hadn't trusted anyone not to file it away as a cold case. He'd sworn to himself that he could stay objective. Look at the facts and not allow his emotions to rule his decisions.

Clearly, he had failed.

"You got anything else for me?" Tom asked through his frustration.

"Actually, I was just getting started," Charlie replied downright cheerfully.

Tom gave him his gaze back and scowled again.

"Whoever this little boy is, dental suggests he was around

twelve to sixteen months old when he passed away. But, for that to be interesting, I should have started with the fact that we got a set of prints. A woman." He swayed his head from side to side. "If I were a betting man, I'd bet that DNA belongs to her."

Finally, good news. *Really* good fucking news, Tom thought as he blew out a heavy breath and settled behind his computer, barking, "Who?"

"Whoa, whoa, whoa… Simmer down. Let me get to why it's interesting."

"Don't fucking—"

"She's dead." Charlie spoke over him. "Killed herself a few years ago. Drove herself into the river with her kids in the car." He paused. "Her son. Her *only* son got out alive."

Tom's whole body locked up. "So, if we got her *only* son in the morgue, who the fuck was the kid in that car?"

Charlie leaned forward, settling his elbows on his knees, and whispered, "I'm guessing Lucas Boyd." He picked the file up and flipped it open. "I vote we pay a little visit to the kid's dad." He scanned the page with his finger then glanced back up. "Porter Reese."

And, with those two simple *words*, Tom exploded from his chair.

# TWENTY-SEVEN

## Charlotte

MY EYES HURT.

My face hurt.

My lungs hurt.

My body hurt.

My brain hurt.

But my heart… It continued to beat in my chest.

Lucas was dead.

And I had to keep living.

Tipping my head back, I caught Porter's blue gaze and whispered, "I think I'm done."

His response was to dip low and kiss me, sad and slow. "How do you feel?" he asked as he pulled away.

"Like shit."

"Is it wrong if I say good?"

I shook my head. "I guess I actually was having a nervous breakdown."

"I think you were more than entitled."

I nodded and looked out at the river. "I'm glad you didn't get eaten by an alligator during yours."

Porter chuckled and pulled me against him so he could kiss my temple. "So, what now?"

I sucked in a deep breath. "Now, we go home and, I guess, plan a funeral for my baby."

His face turned pensive. "I want to be there for you, Charlotte, but I know this is personal. So you have to tell me what you need."

Pushing to my feet, I dusted the back of my jeans off. "I need a glass of wine. I need to call Brady. And then I need to figure out how to move forward with my life. And I want you there for all of that. However, I know *you* need some dry clothes and to go home to your kids."

"Charlotte," he whispered in apology, rising beside me to his full height.

"It's okay. And that's not me pretending." I took his hand and intertwined our fingers, giving him a gentle squeeze. "Why don't I drop you off now? Go home. Start on all of that crap—"

He tugged on my hand. "I don't think you need to be alone."

I stared at him impatiently. "You didn't let me finish. I was going to say start on all of that crap and then come back to your house for that glass of wine tonight after your kids go to bed."

His eyes flared, but a classic Porter Reese smile split his face. "I approve of this plan."

"Good. Now, get naked."

His chin jerked to the side. "I'm sorry. What?"

"I said get naked. There is no way you are getting inside Betty White with wet clothes."

"I'm almost dry!" he defended.

I smiled—on the day when it should have been impossible. But such was life with Porter.

"Then you can *almost* ride in my car."

He groaned.

Minutes later, I laughed as he dug through my trunk, looking for the roll of paper towels that I'd told him were back there.

And then, ten minutes later, after he'd wrapped my driver's seat up like a mummy, we both climbed inside and headed toward his house, leaving a mountain of guilt on the side of that Georgia road.

As Porter drove to his house, I looked at my phone. Two missed calls from Tom. Two from my mom. None from Brady. Assuming he already knew, I didn't find this surprising. I made a mental note to text Mom when I was on my way home. She'd pass the info on to Tom.

Porter and I rode in silence. All the *words* had already been spoken. Well, all except the three that screamed inside my heart. But that wasn't the day for professions of love.

The sun was just starting to go down. Those *words* could wait for another sunrise.

And, for the first time in ten years, I had hope that there would be a lot of sunrises in my future.

"What time do you think you'll be back?" Porter asked when he turned into an upper-middle-class subdivision.

I leaned forward and stared out the windshield as rows of

tall houses started to appear in front of us. They weren't huge like his brother's plantation home, but they were definitely nice. Plush, green grass covered the front yards while tall, dark privacy fences lined the backs. And, from the basketball hoops to the minivans, the place screamed family.

My stomach fluttered, but I didn't allow the panic to set in. This was where Porter lived. There was nothing scary about that.

"Um...what time do your kids go to sleep?" I asked.

"Usually nine, but my mom probably let them stay up until midnight last night, so they probably—" He abruptly stopped talking at the same time his eyes narrowed on something in front of him. "What the fuck?"

I followed his gaze. Two police cars were parked in front of a redbrick two-story just around the bend.

"Is that your house?"

Porter didn't reply as he punched the gas, not slowing until the bottom of my car scraped the bump on his driveway. I cringed at the sound.

He didn't bother cutting the engine before he was out of the car and racing up the sidewalk.

Confused, I stared at his back.

And then the confusion got a whole hell of a lot worse when Tom emerged from inside of his house, a murderous glare contorting his face. His hand shot out and fisted the front of Porter's shirt as he shoved him against the brick wall beside the door.

What the hell?

Slinging my door open, I jumped from the car. "Tom!" I yelled, storming up to the porch.

His irate eyes never lifted to mine as he snatched a pair of cuffs from beneath his blazer.

"Get off me," Porter growled, shoving back before righting himself.

Charlie came jogging out of the house, an older woman with a pale, round face following him. She stopped in the doorway, her mouth opening and closing without actually saying anything, panic dancing in her blue eyes.

"Hey, hey, hey," Charlie said, grabbing Tom's shoulder. "You cannot arrest him. You have nothing to go on."

"Bullshit!" Tom snapped back. "I have enough."

I stepped around the arguing men, my mind reeling, unable to keep up with the chaos. "What the hell are you doing?" I barked, pressing a hand against Tom's chest while doing my best to separate him from Porter.

"Get out of my way, Charlotte," Tom demanded.

"Not until you tell me what's going on!"

His cold, icy gaze swung to mine, and then his whole demeanor gentled as he said, "Lucas isn't dead, babe."

My stomach dropped, and the hairs on the back of my neck stood on end. I stumbled, my back colliding with Porter's front, his arms immediately hooking around my middle.

"What?" I gasped.

"Do not do this until you're sure, Tom," Charlie demanded.

"I'm sure. It's him. You know it as well as I do. Same blood type. Medical history. Everything." Tom's jaw clenched as his gaze flicked over my shoulder to Porter, a menacing snarl forming on his lips. "We have reason to believe that Lucas could be alive and that your boyfriend back there knows where he is."

"What the hell are you talking about?" Porter thundered.

But not a single, solitary word escaped my throat.

My old archnemesis, Hope, made sure of that.

Sticks and stones will break my bones, but words will never harm me.

Lies.

Syllables and letters may not be tangible, but they can still destroy your entire life faster than a bullet from a gun.

One word.

That was all it took to ruin us all.

"Dad?" the little boy called on a broken cry, rushing from around his grandmother and slamming into his father's side.

Seeing as how Porter was flush against my back, it was my side too.

I moved my arm on instinct, but as I dropped it back down, it brushed against the child's back.

I stared at Tom as his eyes got wide, and then they got soft.

Soft the way he looked at me. Soft the way he looked at my mom.

Soft the way he would look at my…son.

Chills exploded across my skin, and my nose began to sting.

Slowly, I slid my gaze down to the little boy at my side. He was staring up at his father, fear etched in his face.

I'd seen Travis before, but right then, with hope tinting my vision, I was looking at him for the very first time.

My straight, raven hair.

His father's dimpled chin.

He wasn't a baby anymore.

He was standing there.

Air in his lungs.

A pulse in his veins.

Alive.

*One word.*

"Lucas," I breathed.

**To be continued in…**

***The Brightest Sunset***
**July 27, 2017**

# OTHER BOOKS

**The Retrieval Duet**

*Retrieval*

*Transfer*

*The Fall Up*

*The Spiral Down*

**The Wrecked and Ruined Series**

*Changing Course*

*Stolen Course*

*Broken Course*

*Among the Echoes*

**On the Ropes**

*Fighting Silence*

*Fighting Shadows*

*Fighting Solutude*

*Savor Me*

**Guardian Protection Series**

*Singe*

# ABOUT THE AUTHOR

Born and raised in Savannah, Georgia, Aly Martinez is a stay-at-home mom to four crazy kids under the age of five, including a set of twins. Currently living in South Carolina, she passes what little free time she has reading anything and everything she can get her hands on, preferably with a glass of wine at her side.

After some encouragement from her friends, Aly decided to add "Author" to her ever-growing list of job titles. So grab a glass of Chardonnay, or a bottle if you're hanging out with Aly, and join her aboard the crazy train she calls life.

Facebook: www.facebook.com/AuthorAlyMartinez

Twitter: twitter.com/AlyMartinezAuth

Goodreads: www.goodreads.com/AlyMartinez